T0304962

BODIES

Christine Anne Foley

JOHN MURRAY

First published in Great Britain in 2024 by John Murray (Publishers)

1

A CIP catalogue record for this title is available from the British Library

Hardback ISBN 9781399807203
Trade Paperback ISBN 9781399807210
ebook ISBN 9781399807227

Typeset in Hoefler Text by Manipal Technologies Limited.

Printed and bound in Great Britain by Clays Ltd, Elcograf S.p.A.

John Murray policy is to use papers that are natural, renewable and recyclable products and made from wood grown in sustainable forests. The logging and manufacturing processes are expected to conform to the environmental regulations of the country of origin.

Carmelite House
50 Victoria Embankment
London EC4Y 0DZ

www.johnmurraypress.co.uk

John Murray Press, part of Hodder & Stoughton Limited
An Hachette UK company

For my Grandparents

I am afraid to own a Body –
I am afraid to own a Soul –
Profound – precarious Property –
Possession, not optional –

Emily Dickinson

YOU

I was chasing something, something not tangible. Something that evaded my grasp and hung in the air. I was envious of the women who looked at you, envious of their curves or their slimness, their breasts or their cheekbones, the pitch of their voice or the rasp of their laughter. I looked at these women and their hair that fell around their faces and I felt my own, my short hair that I tucked behind my ears, my hair that never fell around my face like a movie star or a fictional character in a book. And I hated their vintage clothing, the dress passed down to them by their mother and the swing of their skirts and the looseness of straps on shoulders. And I hated your smile and your open mouth and your teeth all gathered there, lined up and ready, like you would take them and chew them and swallow these women whole.

And you did, you did swallow women whole. You swallowed me whole and I let you and I slipped down easily into your belly and I sat there with the other women and we looked at each other in our chewed-up, digested states and still their hair fell in front of their eyes and still their smiles looked more sophisticated and still my heart raged within me as I was churned and compacted by the muscles of your stomach.

I wake up in cold sweats and I catch myself before I fall from bed and I pull my underwear on and I stand by the window. Then I climb onto my desk and open the window and lean out and let the cool night air encircle me. I could let myself go like this, I could slip out the window and into the night. The wind would carry me and plant me somewhere far away, a place where I wouldn't remember Lar or Johnny or Dave or Kyle or Adam or Con. A place where I wouldn't think about you and your smile and your great, sharkish teeth. Or maybe it wouldn't carry me, maybe I'd be too heavy because of my heavy heart and instead I'd be dragged to the ground by the weight of gravity and I'd land there, and my head would smash from the force of falling, my skull splintered into tiny pieces. And the Guards would come, and they'd take me away and when they'd do the post-mortem, they'd open me up and inside, in there, in my belly would be the half-chewed and digested pieces of all my men. But not you. I never thought of you.

YOU

We met in summer, fifteen years after my first relationship and I instantly knew, this was different. You were different. We met when the days were long and the evenings came in slow, teasing us with the threat of darkness and rain. We sat by the canal with bare legs, fingering the open ends of aluminium cans. The cider was cheap and flat, warmed by our bodies as we carried them in our pockets to our favourite spot. And the grass was sparse and damp. It wet our clothes and when we got home you smelled of outside and tasted like rain.

You didn't play guitar or recite poetry, you didn't get drunk or look at other women. You just sat and ran your hands over my body and your breath was heavy and warm against my cheek.

And I smiled, you know that unconscious smile that doesn't give a warning. The smile that just spreads across your face and you only notice it when your jaw starts to ache and you move fingers to lips to find them spread there, all by themselves, all without your consent.

And we held hands and we walked along the canal, stepping over the outstretched legs of friends and couples and drunks.

And there was music in the air, literally and figuratively. And the low beating from a cheap stereo seeped into our limbs and I don't know if it was the music or the cider, but we felt like we were floating. And the sun was dropping slowly, and a crimson streak stained the sky and birds retreated to their nests in the high branches of trees. And taxis came and went, and revellers flowed to their friends with bags of alcohol, bought in Centra or Aldi, where they'd stood and laughed and argued by the fridge and flashed ID cards and debated mixers and linked arms and discussed the night ahead with fervent enthusiasm.

And I smiled at them too, that uncontrollable grin that was my entire face now, lips to eyes.

Girls in long dresses twirled dangerously close to the water's edge and their boyfriends sat on the lock gates, spreading leather jackets out enticing them to sit down. And some guy would be shouting across the water, arms flailing, starting a chant that would never catch on.

And both sides of the canal would be full now, one side packed with college students clutching cheap bottles of wine and on the other side, young professionals spilling out of the Barge with pints in plastic cups, hanging from a floppy cardboard holder.

And we were voyeurs, merely observing this salad-days rite of passage. We were outsiders, as girls kissed boys and boys kissed boys and girls kissed girls who kissed boys, and lips were cold now as the sun disappeared behind a low-hanging cloud and shadows formed from streetlights that flickered to life behind the bodies.

And the grass felt wet now and the canal darkened and moved languorously, preparing for sleep. And the music felt louder, and the bodies felt warmer and we would soon return home to your place and we would open the bedroom window and the night air would keep us awake and the moon would cast a low light across the end of your bed, illuminating your toes as they brushed against the wooden bed frame.

JOHNNY

The Killers were always playing back then and my hair smelled like Elnett. I wore those tight dresses with the ruched middle, maroon eyeshadow that I had no idea how to apply and shoes with heels that made me walk funny, like I'd polio or something. And I felt bad for thinking it but walking from the car to the pub with the girls, I always did. And they hurt my feet until I was on my third vodka and then I couldn't feel them at all and then I was brave and would talk to him.

I think it was an accident the first night we kissed. An accident for him I mean. He was so drunk but that didn't matter to me, I didn't care. I didn't understand the rule of inebriation back then. At seventeen, I was a novice.

The room was small and warm and by midnight everyone was huddled together by the DJ in the corner and country pubs, Jesus they were claustrophobic as hell, weren't they? I was on the outskirts, looking in at all the cool people, all the girls who'd had sex and had boyfriends and knew what second base meant. And DJ Kelly had that smoke machine, the one that clouded everything up and smelled nice, reminded me of when we did dance shows in school and I stood, vodka glass to my mouth, fingers twirling my hair that felt hard and sticky from the Elnett and I was pretending not to feel alone.

I could see Lorraine dancing with Tom, all curls bouncing. She'd done her hair with her GHD and I wondered if I'd be able to do that. Maybe I would try next weekend, but I didn't have a GHD just a Remington and maybe that wouldn't work. And my mind was full of all these thoughts and the vodka was making them move fast through my brain and I could see myself in her place, all curls dancing and maybe Tom would dance with me then. But he wouldn't, obviously and then Lorraine would be mad anyway so maybe it was for the best. Maybe I'd leave my hair straight and I'd stay on the outskirts.

Then I saw him. Properly. He was talking to his brother Lar who had his arm around some girl with a tattoo on her upper arm and a packet of cigarettes in her hand. She had big breasts, blond hair and a confidence that I couldn't even fathom. And Lar seemed to like her, kept whispering in her ear, and I wondered would anyone ever whisper in my ear. But I knew I'd never get a tattoo and I'd never even tried a cigarette.

Older guys sat at the bar and they drank darker liquor and pints and they talked, and I wondered when you made that transition, when you left the corner with the sticky floor from spilled alcopops and you sat down instead and had, was it deep conversation?

Johnny was so tall and so handsome as he came towards me through the clouded room with his arms out and his grin wide and I should've, I don't know, looked around, checked to see if someone cooler, prettier, stood behind me, but somehow I knew that tonight he was coming for me.

His hands settled on my waist then and he pulled me into the sea of teenagers, all of us drunk on minimal amounts of hard liquor, all dressed up, ridiculously overdone for this small town. Bodies rubbed against my side, my back and my hair kept getting caught in fingers and arms but Johnny kept swinging me from side to side so I brushed it off and swayed with him. And he didn't know the words, but he sang anyway and I laughed and I didn't stop to think why he'd chosen me tonight.

Maybe it was the dress, but this dress was just like all my others. Maybe it was my hair or maybe my breasts were finally coming in. But they weren't, not really. His hair was sort of floppy and I liked it like that, I liked the way he moved his head and his hair followed after, like a guy in a Gillette commercial. And he smelled nice too and when he spun me around I got whiffs of his aftershave but I didn't know the name because I'd never had a boyfriend, not like Lorraine who went to Boots every Christmas and had to pick out a different scent for each new boy.

Johnny was one of the cool guys, he wore a leather jacket and people looked up to him. He only came to school four days a week and his brother, Lar, sold pot and I was just happy to be in his limelight for one night.

Then they played 'Mr Brightside' and that signalled that the night was coming to an end, so he pulled me closer and his breath was on me now, all tobacco and Red Bull and my heart was all kinds of fluttering and skipping and beating. And I moved onto the toes of my ridiculously high polio shoes and he pressed his mouth to mine and he pushed his tongue between my lips. And I just thought about how tongues were so rough and abrasive and how it was weird that we liked to put them in each other. But I kissed him back and I knew he could feel me smiling and his hands were on my bum now and I'm sure he could feel everything through my tight dress and I knew people were watching. Then the lights came up and Lorraine pulled me into the girls' toilets all giggling and laughing.

—Oh my God, oh my God.

I'm smiling too much, too hard.

—Sheila is going to shit a brick.

—What? Why?

—She's been getting with him all month and then last night in O'Reilly's he saw her get with Danny O'Neil and he was so pissed but now, revenge!

Lorraine high-fives me then because we both hate Sheila but suddenly my smile is gone. Now I know why he'd chosen me tonight.

The speaker vibrates against my back as I balance my glass tentatively on my knee, bringing my hand down occasionally to stop it falling off. O'Reilly's is half-empty, we arrived too early and now Cian lies back against the pool table and sighs.

—This is bullshit.

I smile at him, bringing my glass to my lips.

—Wasn't my idea.

I feel Lorraine straighten up in a chair beside me.

—I just wanted to, you know, get out. I was bored cooped up at home. What difference does it make?

I look at Cian again, now hoisting himself onto the table. We both start laughing.

—What?

Lorraine throws her head from side to side.

—What? Go on, say it.

I place my hand on her shoulder.

—Don't worry hun, none of us are going to actually say it.

The not-so-well-kept secret that sat between us was that Lorraine was here to see Tom Doyle.

—He's . . . all elbows.

Cian looks towards the bar as he says it.

—What does that even mean?

Lorraine seems annoyed.

—Just, I dunno, clumsy or something.

Tom is sitting on a high stool surrounded by friends, all holding pints to their chests in what appears to be some sort of reverent silence.

—I just think they're . . . boring?

I say it like a question.

Lorraine furrows her brow.

—Sorry, maybe he's nice.

I turn away from Tom and his friends and see Lorraine blushing.

—He is.

—Well then, never mind his elbows or his . . . dullness.

I raise my glass and Cian hops off the pool table to clink glasses.

—Yeah, sorry hun.

He kisses Lorraine's forehead.

Slowly the pub starts to fill and groups come to play pool, glasses left on our table.

—Lucky we aren't roofers.

Cian thinks his sexual assault joke is funny but myself and Lorraine launch into a discussion about rape culture. It isn't until much later that Lar and his crew arrive. We feel it before we even see them, a shift in everyone's energy. The boss is in town. The pool table is swiftly vacated even though Lar is at the bar ordering drinks, but nobody wants to be the one asked to move. We are still sitting in our spot, five drinks in at this point and Lorraine takes her hair down, swings it back and forth vying for Tom Doyle's attention.

—Go talk to him,

Cian is insisting but Cian is drunk and doesn't understand the perils of such a move.

—What if he tells her to fuck off?

They both look at me now.

—Why would he do that?

Lorraine looks hurt, upset.

—Well, like, he won't but, he could.

—Why?

Cian asks while he pulls a box of cigarettes from his pocket and places them on the table.

—Okay, well not that but like . . . I dunno, I just wouldn't have the balls.

—Yeah but you're little innocent Charlotte, Lorraine is a different species.

We all laugh and I agree but I feel my face go red.

In the end Tom Doyle comes to speak to us. He approaches confidently and I nudge Lorraine.

—See now, isn't this much better than you chasing him?

But she isn't listening, too busy tying her hair back up. He introduces himself to us and not long after takes Lorraine to the bar for a drink.

Cian looks at me long and hard across the table, tutting.

—What? You were all for that a minute ago.

He gives me a patronising smile.

—I know, the tut-tutting is for you. When are we going to get you a man?

I return his look with an equally patronising one of my own. Reaching across the table I place my hand on his hand and say

—and when are we going to get one for you?

Then in one swift movement I grab his packet of cigarettes and hold them in the air like a trophy.

—You bitch,

he cries and jumps up, grabbing the cigarettes from my fingers.

—The men of Coolfarnamanagh are not ready for Cian O'Shea. Actually, I might go out and have one. You'll be okay here?

I nod.

—Yes, maybe a prince will come and kiss me, and I'll turn into a frog and then he can take me to his tower and rape me.

—That's some fucked-up fairy-tale you have there.

—Aren't they all?

I sit back laughing and sip my vodka orange. R.E.M. beats a rhythm on my back and I wonder why this DJ plays the same old shit every week. Then I wonder why we come here every week. It is as I'm mulling this over that I hear a commotion down the back. A row is breaking out and unsurprisingly, Lar Casey, Johnny's brother, is at its centre. Some guy I don't recognise is holding Lar back, Lar's broad shoulders bursting through his thin t-shirt.

That's when I see Johnny, he swoops in and stands in front of Lar. A smile has spread onto Lar's lips and he's laughing at his rival. Johnny waves his arms, asking both to calm down and I notice such a difference in them. Johnny is smaller in stature, hair floppier, and his face is more serious. Lar's face is weathered, holds character and there's a confidence to how he carries himself. Johnny is confident too but it's more forced. He pulls his shoulders up, puffs his chest out and frowns at Lar's opponent. Lar lowers himself into a chair behind him and the other guy is dragged away by a group of friends. Lar wipes his mouth with the back of his hand and for a minute it looks like he might spit onto the floor, lip bleeding from a blow to the face. Johnny turns around and gestures to the barman, who comes running with a pint of water. Lar dips his fingers into the glass and pulls out two ice cubes, shakes them and places them to his lip. Johnny pats his shoulder and looks around. He's looking for his friends. He's looking for Sheila Ryan.

I turn back to my empty table now that the commotion has come to an end, the night's theatrics over, and I pull out an ice cube from my glass. I hold it between my fingers and watch as the ice melts against my skin. I bring the ice to my face and feel the sharp coldness of it on my mouth.

—Charlotte.

I look up and see Johnny standing at my table. His eyes are wide, lips too and he sits down on Lorraine's chair.

—Johnny.

I smile as I say his name and drop the ice cube back into my glass.

—How the fuck are you?

He seems pleased to see me and I relax a little in my seat.

—I'm good, yeah, not bad.

—Good, good. Jesus, did you see all that carry-on over there.

I nod.

—Fucking mental. I was like, boys, get the fuck away from my brother.

I smile.

—Oh yeah?

—Yeah and they were all, fuck you, I'll do you and I was like, who even are you? They're from Kilmont or some shithole, like fuck off.

—What do they have against your brother?

I look to the bar and see Lar being bought drinks and his crew drooling over him.

—I dunno, some shite from ages ago. All bullshit.

All drugs, I'm thinking.

—So, yeah, anyway, you uh, you look unreal. Like really nice.

I look down at my top and I smile, embarrassed by the sudden change in conversation.

—I wanted to, you know, mention about the other night.

Oh fuck.

—That was . . .

A mistake? An accident? The most awful thing that had ever happened and he hadn't slept since due to the intense revulsion he felt at the thought of touching my arse in O'Donovan's.

—That was really nice.

I look really nice. The other night was really nice. Everything was really nice.

I put my fingers back into my glass for lack of something to do and I push the melted ice around.

—Yeah, yeah, I thought it was nice too.

Johnny smiles and moves his chair closer to me.

—You're a really good kisser.

He moves his hand onto my shoulder then up around my neck and then he's touching my ear. His arms are so tanned in his rolled-up white shirt and there's sweat on his upper lip from defending his brother. He moves his face to mine and I can almost taste him, taste the beer and the cologne and the desire on his breath. Then he gently places his lips against mine and pulls my body into his and we are kissing now, and I can hear a cheer from someone deep in the pub and I don't know if it's Cian or Lorraine or some random person doing a random cheer but I'm smiling again and I know he can feel it.

When he eventually pulls away he's smiling too and he rubs his hands together.

—Can I get you a drink?

I look at the table, at my empty glass of vodka but for some reason I say

—Ah no, I'm grand.

—You sure? Alright then, sure I better go see the patient, you know.

He nods his head in the direction of Lar at the bar and I say

—Oh yeah, you better.

And I give the most embarrassing, feeble laugh.

As soon as he leaves, I see Cian and Lorraine appear from the shadows like the resurrected Christ.

—Oh my fucking God. Two weekends in a row!

Lorraine seems very pleased with the progress of my minor romance.

—He's so fucking buff.

Lorraine and I look at Cian for a definition of the word buff.

—Ugh, you're all so straight. He's hot, like.

We nod in agreement and I bring my fingers to my lips once more but this time they feel warm, there is no cold sharpness.

When the DJ finishes for the night, Lorraine declares starvation and we agree to take her to the chipper. I look around the bar for Johnny. He's no longer with his brother who now sits with his girlfriend, hand resting on her bare thigh. He's not at the pool table and Cian tells me he's not outside smoking.

We grab our jackets and make our way out into the cool night air. Cian runs into the street, throwing his arms up and howling at the sky.

—We really must get rid of him.

Lorraine puts on an English accent and puts her arm around me laughing.

We queue up in the chipper and are about to order when Lorraine gasps, clasps her hand to her mouth and stares outside.

—What's wrong? You caught sight of your own reflection?

I'm laughing at Cian's joke while my eyes follow Lorraine's gaze and that's when I stop laughing. Outside, up against Lar Casey's Renault Megane, Johnny Casey is kissing Sheila Ryan, holding one of her legs around his waist and one of his hands not visible.

—That fucking slut.

Lorraine is outraged.

—She must have been down in O'Donovan's.

—Don't slut-shame the girl, he's the slut here.

I agree with Cian and I know he's right.

I turn away from the door and I lean over the greasy counter.

—Three curry chips, please.

Then I turn back to the window and murmur

—Yes actually, he's the fucking slut.

LAR

The sun hangs half mast in the sky as we sit by the river and there's a chill in the air so I rub my legs ferociously, making the blood circulate and the goose bumps disappear. The can is cold when I bring it to my lips and the cider is flat, tastes almost sour but I swallow it and my cheeks feel warmer with each sip.

When we finish, I gather up the empty cans and pile them into an old Lidl bag for life.

—Lads, c'mon, we're not animals.

Lorraine is already skipping off down the line with the others, twirling and singing. Barry stays back to help me. He passes me some cans and his hands are cold but feel kind of damp and sweaty, like that one kid nobody wanted to hold hands with in primary school. He starts to make small talk and I know that he fancies me, but I just can't bring myself to reply. Instead, I stand up sharply as a flock of crows flies out from the woods across the river and their sound ricochets.

—They do that at the same time every evening.

Barry looks at me unbelieving but I'm smiling as I watch the birds swoop up and down in the sky above our heads. They fill the air with cawing and when they disappear it feels strangely silent. The river is low and quiet and looks so peaceful now that the rest of our pack have left and can be barely heard in the distance, faint laughing and speaking. I walk closer to the bank and watch the water, every now and then a ripple appearing, something moving under its dark skin.

—We should probably . . .

Barry gestures towards the others who have left the river path and can be seen, tiny dots at the entrance to town. I nod and follow him, and I feel kind of bad for being so rude but it's difficult. I don't like him that way and when he looks at me it's painful, like he's trying so hard and it makes me uncomfortable. I'm about to say something generic about the cider or the weather when he reaches out and puts his arm around my shoulder.

I stop walking and look at him.

—Lar's crew are up there.

He looks at the ground as he says it.

—And?

—And I'm protecting you.

—Putting your arm around me is hardly protection now, is it?

We are just at the entrance to town now and I look up and see Lar's crew sitting on the fence. They're passing a cigarette around, although I'm thinking it's probably weed. Lar sits in the middle wearing a grey top and torn jeans. His hair is jet black and matches his dark eyes that look out under a dense hood of eyebrows. His skin, too, is dark, like he always has a tan, and his fingers look rough as he brings the joint to his lips.

—You're trying to show off, Barry, and it's totally not cool.

I bring my hand to my shoulder and pull his arm away. I watch it swing down by his side and I realise I've been quite forceful. I walk ahead then and towards the gate. Two of Lar's crew jump down as I near the gate but Lar stays sitting on it.

—Magic word.

He inhales the joint and then blows it out towards my face. The smell is sweet, familiar.

I'm annoyed now. Annoyed at Lorraine for going ahead without me, annoyed at Barry for being a prick and annoyed at Lar for being so stupid and bossy and good-looking.

—I dunno, you're a big cunt?

It comes out of my mouth before I realise I've said it.

Lar's face changes then and he slides down from the fence. He grins at me and opens the gate.

—That's four words but still, correct.

I look up at him as I walk past. His grin is wide, teeth yellowing, but Jesus he has a handsome face.

—Thanks.

I say it as he curtsies, and I hear the rest of the group laughing.

Lar's breath is hot and smells of Sambuca and tobacco and it tickles my neck when he moves his head close to me. He speaks into the fold of my shoulder so I edge closer to him to relieve the sensation.

My head is now nuzzling his collarbone and his hand is lightly resting on the small of my back. His girlfriend is inside and so is Johnny and all of this is wrong and immoral and just totally unbelievable. It's unbelievable that Lar would have ever looked at me across the pub, ever rubbed his hand along my seat, brushing my thigh. It's unbelievable that after weeks of this back and forth I would follow him outside and we would now be standing in the shadows, wrapped in each other, wrapped in this sin.

We don't speak about it. Lar doesn't speak much at all.

—Oi, Murphy, I can see your thong,

he'd shouted at me as I left O'Donovan's about a month before and I'd blushed and watched as the crew laughed and Lorraine had told him to go fuck himself and put her arm around my shoulder and said softly

—He's just a wanker.

But I'd turned around and looked at him, big Lar Casey, Johnny's brother, standing there with a cigarette between his lips and both hands swinging by his sides and I'd watched as the cigarette dropped slightly and a smile spread across his lips.

Lar's hand is on my head now and he pulls my hair lightly so that my head tips back and my eyes stare up at him. He brings his mouth to mine with a tenderness that I will never be able to recreate with anyone else. A tenderness about which I will never be able to tell anyone. And he lifts my body, so much smaller than his, until my legs are around his waist and he pushes me hard against the wall and I think this may be the sexiest thing that has ever happened to me. And I forget about his girlfriend who has the big tits that make her top crease in the middle and I forget about his brother and the coarse feel of his tongue in my mouth and I forget about how I haven't shaved my legs properly on the thigh and how he can probably feel them, and I forget about my rouge lips and how they are staining his face and I forget the time and the day and the year and I am lost in him.

His hands are rough and they scratch my skin and his lips are cracked and I can taste the flesh of them and I can taste him and I like the taste. I like the Sambuca and the tobacco and I like the danger of it all.

When we stop kissing my head is light and I'm dizzy. Lar places me back on the ground gently and his hands slide from my waist to my shoulder and he grins and looks at his feet and we don't speak because there is nothing to be said. And I throw one foot back onto the wall and lean back and try to remain calm though my heart beats fast in my chest.

—I better . . .

he says and his head nods in the direction of the pub and suddenly I realise how near we are and how risky this is as we stand down the lane, behind a low wall. And I nod and say something like

—I'll follow you a bit later.

And I let him walk away and I swallow hard and I press the back of my head against the wall and I feel the cold of it and I can taste the tobacco on my lips and I feel that maybe I want a cigarette and the following month when I see his girlfriend with the big tits that make her shirt crease in the middle wearing a top that now pulls tight across her rounded belly I have that first cigarette.

Lar wears this gold chain that sits on a pale line of skin around his neck and as summer blossoms his tan appears around it like a line of rust. His hair is always slicked back, wet-looking from the wax and a few strands always come undone and sit on his forehead, greasy to the touch. His lips are big and always dry, cracked and he licks them when he's thinking. His hands are rough but they contain a feeling of security and when he holds me I feel safe.

I wonder if he is like this with other people. Is he like this with his girlfriend? Or is he more rough then, more big-man-Lar with her than this soft soul he is with me? Or am I just hoping that I am somehow special?

I mean, I guess I am special, in a sense. In the sense that nobody knows about me, about us, special in the sense that nobody ever can.

—You're gorgeous, like.

His voice is low, gruff and he barely looks at me when he says it. I don't necessarily enjoy the compliments, they make me uneasy.

—Ha ha, yeah.

I wave a fly from my face and he brings his hand to me. The roughness moves along my cheek, fingers graze my lips.

—No, like, seriously.

I shake my head. I'm not sure why. Am I shaking away the comment or the truth of it or am I just finding something to do.

—We shouldn't be . . .

I don't finish it. I don't need to.

—It's complicated.

He says it as he looks at the ground, his favourite place to look when he isn't searching my face.

—Exactly.

I say it loud, definite and we both know what I mean, both know I'm talking about the swell of his girlfriend's belly and the life that grows inside it.

—But it's different.

And I nod because I know what he means then too. It's different because I'm new, I'm younger, I'm innocent. It's different because I haven't had a boyfriend, nobody looks at me, speaks of me. It's different mainly because he hasn't fucked me and isn't sure if he ever will.

I lean against the wall. I'm always leaning against walls when I'm with Lar.

—I really, really like you.

I know he does. I know there's truth in that.

—I really like you too.

—Well then.

And his eyes move back from the ground and back to my eyes and he's grinning now and he says

—Then there's no matter.

And I nod and I smile and he kisses me and he holds me and I feel like the world has stopped and I feel like I'm spinning.

There's no matter. Except of course, there is.

I was drunk and that was my excuse and that was no excuse at all, but Lorraine and Cian were egging me on and I couldn't exactly tell them about Lar anyway.

And Johnny was handsome, Johnny was single and Johnny didn't have some girl knocked up and Johnny wasn't a drug dealer and Johnny wasn't . . . Lar. But Johnny was Lar's brother and I knew there to be some sort of moral code around that. I suppose that wasn't really okay but then none of it was. It wasn't okay that Lar had winked at me across the bar when his girlfriend went to the bathroom. It wasn't a surprise to anyone when they broke up. It wasn't a surprise to me. It wasn't the first time and it wouldn't be the last. Lar was that type of guy. The type to have multiple kids with different girls. The type to go after big-titted, tattooed girls. The type to always have 'on and off' girlfriends but who would never be seen with me. We were too different, our lives too far apart.

But he was with her all the time he was with me and he was as lost as me, and he was as frustrated as me and he didn't really love me now did he? He couldn't have, he barely knew me.

And I thought Lar would kill Johnny that night, his own brother who didn't know what crime he'd committed. But he didn't, because he couldn't. But he was mad. Or was he impressed or what kind of feeling did he have at all?

—Char he's fucking looking at you.

Lorraine's eyes are big and she spins on her stool and I have to keep slapping her thigh telling her to shut up because Johnny will hear.

She looks at me and says

—But I want him to hear. I want Sheila to hear.

And this would have annoyed me. This would have royally pissed me off if it wasn't for Lar. If it wasn't for those secret moments down the Pitch and Putt and the light touch of Lar's coarse hands and the secrets that those trees above us held. This would have annoyed me a few weeks ago, or was it months, months ago when I first caught Lar's glance when he called after me.

—Oi, Murphy, I can see your thong.

And all the girls told me he was a wanker and

—Are you okay?

and

—Don't mind him Char.

But I saw the cigarette droop between his lips and I saw that look on his face and I knew.

So I was no longer jealous of Sheila Ryan and I was no longer looking at Johnny Casey because I'd seen Lar Casey drop to his knees and I'd felt Lar Casey's hand on my back and Lar Casey's tongue in my mouth so I shrugged and I rolled my eyes and I drank more vodka diluted with cordial and I sang along to Gwen Stefani and I stood underneath the smoke machine and coughed and laughed and every five minutes I looked to the door to see if Lar was coming in.

And I was drunk then, and I wanted to text Lar but we rarely did, so I looked at my phone and I saw that there were no messages and I knew he was home with her. 'On' again, then. And I imagined him running the long fingers of his rough hands down her swollen belly and I imagined her stupid laugh and his beautiful lips and his big smile and I was angry, I was raging. I was jealous. And then Johnny, Johnny Casey, Lar's brother, came up to me through the smoke again and this time I knew it wasn't my dress or my hair, but more importantly I knew it wasn't to make Sheila Ryan jealous, this time he was coming for me. He was coming for me because of Lar. Now he didn't know. He didn't know about us and he wouldn't but he could sense something, something about me had changed. Lorraine had noticed it too, a sort of shift in me, a sort of newness.

—Well look at fucking you.

Which was Lorraine's way of giving a compliment.

And I could feel it myself. I could feel the warmth of it. I could feel it radiate out of me and into the pub. And what was it then, a confidence? I don't know but it was a strong enough force to pull Johnny Casey towards me and he had me up against the galvanised fence with his tongue jabbing at my mouth when I felt my phone buzz in my skirt pocket. And his mouth was clumsy and not like Lar's and he wasn't a bad kisser, but the kisses weren't like Lar's and when I pulled my phone out as he came up for air, I saw Lar's name on my screen and he was saying

—I'm in O'Donovan's.

And my heart went of a flutter and I thought I'd get sick and Johnny was looking at me but that was it; it was just at me, not into me, not like Lar did. And he was grinning, and it was just like Lar's grin, but I could see his teeth and I hated him, and I hated his teeth and then I could imagine Lar coming out, out the back of O'Donovan's and seeing us there. And he'd come down the lane and he'd smash his own brother's teeth in and his girlfriend would be standing in the doorway looking at me and a crowd would form behind her and they'd be looking at me and then everyone would know. But then Johnny's phone rang, and it was the boys and he said

—We'd better go in

and I wanted to say

—I'll follow in a minute

just like I said to Lar that first night, but I couldn't because there was no sense to me standing out in the cold on my own. So we headed back in, me and Johnny Casey, Lar's brother, and there were whoops from the boys and they patted Johnny's back like he'd completed a marathon or something, not roughly jammed his tongue down some young one's throat. And Lar was at the bar and he saw us come in and he heard the cheers and he knew Johnny hadn't completed a marathon. So he stood there with a pint in his hand and his girlfriend rubbed his back and then her belly and I was thinking to myself how she was too pregnant to be in a pub when I realised that I had no fucking right to judge. And when I looked at Lar he turned away and I felt sick then and I went to the bathroom and it all came rushing out of me in a hot, acidic stream.

And later that night when Lar pushed me up against the pebble-dashed wall behind the chipper he shoved his hand hard up my skirt and it was the first time he had touched me there, it was the first time anyone had touched me there and he said

—Does Johnny do that?

and I shook my head and I knew he didn't taste the sick on my breath or if he did, he didn't care.

Lar Casey was the first man I held in my hands. And I knew it was disgraceful and I thought it then and I suppose I think it now, disgraceful that the first penis I touched had put life inside another woman, another woman who was sitting inside drinking Fanta, waiting for her boyfriend to return from his overly long trip to the bathroom.

I remember Lar Casey's penis to this very day. I remember it better than anyone else's because it surprised me so much. I'm not sure what I'd been expecting but I think it must have been a big, firm thing that sat rigid between my fingers because that's what they talk about. They mention the blood flow and the hardness of a penis, but they never mention the weight of it but my God, I'll never forget the weight of Lar Casey. I looked down at this unyielding thing that lay large and warm and heavy in my hands. And as I wrapped my fist around it, I felt its expectance, its whole purpose looking up at me, to be tugged and pulled. As expectant and eager as Lar himself. And Lar's hips moved in tandem with my hand and it was in this moment and the moments that followed when Lar exploded hot, sticky residue onto my fingers, it was in these moments that I realised how bodies controlled us, how our bodies were not merely vessels but in fact dictators with their own resolve.

JOHNNY

Johnny drove fast, too fast and I'm not sure if I felt unsafe or excited. I did, however, feel guilty and there was a sort of pain in my stomach that lingered. It had been there for days and my mother had given me Alka-Seltzer and my dad had recommended some herbal shite but the pain didn't go because the pain wasn't real.

Anxiety can cause physical symptoms. Stomach pain. Weakness or fatigue. Headaches. Rapid breathing. Nausea.

Google. But Google didn't know a thing because this wasn't anxiety, and this wasn't what you'd call stomach pain or nausea. This was a deep, haunting feeling that dwelled in the depths of me and no amount of slow breathing or mindfulness would shift it.

It felt, I imagined, like a spoiled pregnancy. One you'd read about in the *Woman's Way* magazine where the baby died and the mother knew before any doctor told her. That's how I felt. Like a baby had died. Like a life had been lost inside me.

But I knew I wasn't pregnant, unless it was an immaculate conception. Unless you could get pregnant from touching Lar Casey with your hand, but even I knew that couldn't happen.

So I looked at Johnny as he drove and I smiled out the window and I couldn't really believe that here I was in a car with Johnny fucking Casey but I couldn't even enjoy it because I could still hear his brother's words in my ears.

—You're gorgeous, like.

And I pulled the visor down in the passenger seat and I looked at my reflection in the little rectangle mirror and I thought, Jesus, I'm really not.

And I wasn't. My eyebrows were thin and I'd drawn them on and they didn't look like the girls you'd see on Facebook and my lipstick was too bright, but I always wore red and maybe it aged me but wasn't that what I wanted? And the eyeliner was all wrong, it always was, and my hair was just . . .

—Charlotte?

I look up and see that we've stopped. We've pulled in to some cul-de-sac and Johnny's speaking to me but I'm too lost in my own face, my own flaws.

—Sorry.

He laughs.

—You look lovely.

No. I look gorgeous. I look gorgeous, like.

We get out of the car then and we walk towards a wooden gate. Johnny hoists himself onto it and he's grinning. A big fat grin that makes his cheeks swell and Jesus, the truth is, he is the one who is gorgeous. And I look at his legs as he climbs and his bare ankles and the swell of his arse in those tight jeans and I see his hips move and I feel my heart race and I want to slap myself.

—For fuck's sake, Charlotte.

He stops climbing then and turns around.

—You alright?

And I've spoken aloud and I'm embarrassed.

—Just, I'm not really dressed for this.

I gesture down at my black miniskirt and I pull my jumper down to cover it a bit and I feel fucking dumb.

—I'll help.

And then it occurs to me that maybe this was his plan. Maybe picking a gate like this was his plan all along and as I throw my legs over the gate, his hands reach up until he's touching my thighs and as I slip down on the other side his hand grazes my arse and I'm glad and embarrassed at the same time that I'm wearing a thong.

I wonder if my arse is particularly hairy or if the unevenness I feel is cellulite or goose bumps from the cold and I run my hand along the skin as I walk behind him through this conclave of trees and I'm not even wondering where we are going because I'm so wrapped up in trying to figure out what Johnny Casey might have felt, what he might be thinking.

We make it through the trees and come to a sort of opening and all the time he's walking in front of me and he's pulling brambles and all sorts of branches out of my way by reaching his arm back and I can't stop looking at the skin taut on his muscles and maybe I'm ovulating or something because this can't be normal. I think he's a beautiful specimen and I imagine him naked and I imagine his body coming out of the shower and how the water must cling to it, the droplets hanging onto him for dear life because how could they ever want to leave.

But then we finally stop as we come to the opening and we're standing in a big field with a huge derelict house, and I remember it slightly because I've definitely been here before.

And we wander the rooms of this empty house and the quiet of it surrounds us and we are intruding. And I think of fairy rings and I feel a shiver and I grab Johnny's shoulders when there's the squeak of a mouse and he laughs and he puts his arm around me.

And then I'm turning in to him and he folds his body into mine and his lips run along my jaw and onto my mouth and we stand here in this carcass of a house and he kisses me and it's better this time, better than out the back of O'Donovan's. And in this moment the horrible anxious feeling vanishes and I genuinely feel gorgeous, like.

LAR

Johnny drove Lar's car. Johnny sat in the driver's seat with his tanned legs sticking out of grey shorts while he held my hand over the handbrake, Lar's handbrake. Johnny took Sheila Ryan's virginity in the back seat of that car.

Johnny loved Sheila Ryan. That was the word on the street. Johnny loved Sheila Ryan and that made him take her tight-fitting blouse off in the back of Lar's Renault Megane.

I'd been spending every Thursday evening with him that summer. He'd pulled up in Lar's car and picked me up and we'd driven out to the old house and we'd kissed and we'd told each other stories and he'd tried to put my hand down his trousers and I'd pulled my hand away because I didn't want to do that or I didn't know how because the only person I'd ever done that to was Lar. And I didn't see Lar much that summer. He was busy, his girlfriend had a baby and he'd broken up with her two days later and everyone hated him, and I hated him because I didn't hear from him for weeks. And I messaged him one Saturday night when the rain fell so hard on my Velux window that I thought it was going to break, and I'd come in from the pub and I'd had too many vodkas and said something like

—Well

Which was as much a declaration as it was a question or a greeting. And I lay there in my clothes waiting for the blue ticks to appear so I'd know he'd read it, while the rain came down and I nearly wished the window would smash open and I'd drown.

So I started meeting Johnny, and Lorraine was worried because Lorraine knew what Johnny was like and she thought that I just wasn't cool enough for him. And he did the predictable thing where he ignored me in public and I pretended to Lorraine that I didn't care, and I pretended to myself that I didn't notice, and he followed Sheila Ryan around the pub and she ignored him. And I know what people would have said, if I'd had the balls to tell them how I felt when the stories of back-seat shenanigans came into the pub, they'd have said, wasn't I the bigger fool, and of course I was.

So I cried myself to sleep the night Johnny's friend, Paul, who was sleeping with Lorraine, told her about Sheila and Johnny, because I'd been out with Johnny the day before and I'd let him rub my breasts under my bra. I cried, not because I cared about Johnny Casey, not because I wished it was me in the back seat but because I realised, and how the realisation only came me to me then I'll never know, but I realised that I'd never been in Lar's car with anyone else other than Johnny Casey. I'd never been in Lar's car with Lar.

And then Lar texted me. Weeks later, maybe months, I can't remember, but the leaves on the trees were falling and I had moved to Dublin to study Arts and I was in college now and I was looking out over the foyer in Trinity Halls and he said

—Well

and it was as much a declaration as it was a question or a greeting and the next thing I knew we were back and we were looking into each other's eyes and he lay in bed beside me and he said

—I love you.

And I still hadn't slept with him and he still hadn't really tried but he'd gone down there between my legs and I'd laughed and I'd cried and then he told me he was back with the mother of his child.

And I wasn't angry. Not properly because how could I be? He had a child, he had responsibilities and anyway, he loved me. How could I be angry with someone who loved me? He told me that Sheila had broken up with Johnny because she was going to college in Cork.

And every weekend I'd go home and I'd see him in the pub and I'd see Johnny and I was moving on I suppose, because I didn't seem to care until one night he came up to me and he said

—I love you

again.

And I fell back and this would happen again and again and he'd touch me and I'd lose my balance and suddenly I was cool and Sheila Ryan was fat and nobody wanted to do anything with her in the back seat of a Renault Megane or any other car now, because in rural Ireland in 2003, being skinny was the main benchmark for attractiveness.

But we couldn't be, and we weren't, not in the end and Lar stayed with his girlfriend. But he'd approach me in the pub and he'd touch my hair and tell me about his baby.

—Ah he's *gorgeous*.

And the word would fall heavy from his mouth and I hated it because it meant nothing now, now that it wasn't about me. And then he'd say

—I look at us, the three of us and I think to myself, that could've been me and you and our baby.

Then he tucks my hair behind my ear, and we stand outside O'Donovan's and we aren't hiding beneath the trees of the Pitch and Putt or at the back of the library. We aren't sneaking in and out of Trinity Halls late at night. We are standing firmly side by side, old friends, and nobody could question it although they probably did.

—When did Charlotte Murphy get so tight with Lar Casey?

—Ah sure wasn't she doing a line back in the day with his brother, the younger fella, Johnny?

And they'd be right.

They described the incident as tragic.

The Renault Megane had gone flying off down Timmy Mahony's lane and into the ditch and Johnny had died on impact in the passenger seat and Lar died later in hospital, his now-fiancée standing over him, his child by her side, clutching her by the hand.

And the papers wrote about it for weeks, about how the child would grow up fatherless and my mother passed some comment like

—Wouldn't he have anyway

And I'd slammed a door in the house protesting her bitterness.

Lar's body lay still in the coffin and his brother lay in the one beside him and it was tragic or a travesty and aren't they the same thing anyway? And Sheila Ryan wore a black dress because she'd gotten back with Johnny and she did big gulps and her eyes gave birth to fat tears. And I stood with Lorraine and she touched my arm because she knew I had

—a fondness for the young O'Casey

and she knew this regardless of

—how much of a prick he was.

But she didn't know about Lar. She didn't know how I'd gone to the wake and looked at him there and saw how he'd looked like he was sleeping and how they'd taken the gold chain off his neck, a pale line of whiteness choking him. And she didn't know that I'd run my hand across his brow, felt the coldness creep into my fingers, up my hand, my arm and into my core. A coldness that stayed with me for days. She didn't know that I'd felt the papery texture of his flesh and how I hadn't cried, not once since my mother had come home to tell me. How she'd sat me down and told me all about poor Johnny Casey and then added at the end

—And wasn't it Lar who was driving, of course. And he's in ICU and Jesus I'm not wishing him any harm but . . .

And she never finished the sentence, but I knew what she meant because nobody had much time for Lar at all.

I suppose they didn't know the tenderness. They didn't know how he'd touched the small of my back with a lightness that could lift me. They didn't know of his lips and how they stirred me. They didn't know of his stories and his dreams and how he wanted his world to be. They saw a pot dealer, a chain-smoker, a knocker-upper and I couldn't tell them any different because if I had, they would have asked how I knew, and then they'd have called him a cheater and me a whore.

SAOIRSE

When Saoirse got a job on the beauty counter in Boots she said she was so happy she might die. She came home every evening with a new lotion or potion claiming to change your face or your belly or your legs and turn you into a supermodel.

—This lipliner is life-changing.

Saoirse sits on the floor of my bedroom emptying a huge make-up bag onto the carpet.

—What's a lipliner?

—Seriously? It's in the name Char. It lines the lips.

—Do we need to line our lips?

I join her on the floor and start rifling through the stash. Saoirse slaps my hand hard.

—Saoirse, Jesus.

—Stop swearing. And stop breaking everything.

—I'm not breaking anything.

—Well you might, with your big clutsy hands.

—Clutsy is not a word.

Saoirse opens a palette with a mirror and rubs her lips.

—Oh sorry, Kafka. Do you want to learn how to look nice or do you want to end up like Moira Rourke, going on sixteen and not even as much as a look from a boy. Anyway, I need you to be my guinea pig, come here.

—I dunno.

—It wasn't a question Charlotte.

When Saoirse finishes, she tells me to close my eyes.

—I'm bringing in the good mirror for the big reveal. Stay here and do not look at yourself or I will rip Lily's head off.

Saoirse leaves and I open my eyes, checking that my beloved Lily the lamb is still safe on my bed.

—She doesn't mean it,

I turn and reassure Lily.

I close my eyes again and Saoirse comes in.

—Okay, okay. Are you ready?

—No.

—Shut up. And open your eyes, you degenerate.

I look at myself as Saoirse balances the good mirror on her knee.

—Well?

I bring my hand to my face.

—I look . . .

—Way better than you normally do?

—No, like a prostitute from a Dickens novel.

Saoirse throws the mirror to one side.

—My God. Moira Rourke will have nothing on you. You'll be a virgin 'til you're fifty.

—Don't give up the day job, that's all I'm saying Saoirse.

—This is my day job you idiot.

When she leaves, I go to the bathroom to remove the make-up but for a few minutes I look at myself in the mirror. My cheeks are rosy, my brows suddenly pronounced. My lips are a crimson red and I try a pout. Ridiculous but kind of grown-up, kind of beautiful. I stare at myself for ten minutes.

—Knew you liked it.

Saoirse leans against the bathroom door.

—Have you ever heard of privacy? Get out!

Later that night, I'm lying in bed with a Meg Cabot novel and Saoirse comes in and jumps up beside me.

—*Princess Diaries?*

I nod.

—Any prostitutes in that?

—Not yet anyway.

—Disappointing. Give me.

I pass the book to Saoirse and she starts to read. I rest my head against her and she puts her arm around me.

—See, she has a lovely boyfriend.

I smile.

—I know, and his neck smells amazing.

—His neck?

—Apparently.

—Lucky bitch.

We fall asleep together like this and in the middle of the night Saoirse wakes up and pushes me off her.

—You snore like a dog.

She gets up to go to her own room but on the way out she turns around and places a small tube on my dresser.

—Less whoreish. A light gloss for babies like you.

When she leaves I get up and look at the lipgloss, 'Juicy Tube'. I open the lid and apply gloss to my lips. Definitely not whoreish.

YOU

Quinns is packed, heaving. Warm bodies pressed against each other. The smell of cider, sweat, anticipation and fear. A sea of blue and white, black and amber, thick necks above jersey collars, Setanta playing highlights on the giant screen. Loud voices, cheering, cajoling. Groups of friends in Dublin for the All-Ireland weekend, their cheeks sunburned from a day at Croke Park, now even pinker and more flushed from daytime drinking.

I approach the bar in my loose-fitting black dress, one of the few people in the pub not wearing their county's colours, never one to go in for the patriotism of the day, but always ready to show up for the social. I'd come to meet my cousin Laura and her boyfriend after the match. Kilkenny had won and Laura and Sam were deep in debate about who should have won Man of the Match.

—C'mon now Char, is he talking sense?

—Not getting involved, going to the bar.

I wave my hands and walk away listening to Sam say

—No but, seriously, seriously.

41

The bar is crowded and I squeeze myself through the cracks between limbs to get closer. I reach my fingers out and grip the sticky counter, pulling my body under somebody's arm.

—Really? You're going to do that?

As I fix myself to the bar I look up.

—I mean, it's impressive.

You look down at me, eyes wide, a half-smile on your lips.

—There are few benefits to being five foot nothing so I'm definitely going to utilise the ones I can, okay?

Your smile turns to a grin.

—That's fair but I'm still going to get served before you.

I shake my head and laugh.

—How so?

—Well. I'm taller, and I can make hand gestures and signals above your head. So, say I was trying to order . . . what are you drinking?

—Orchard Thieves.

—Say I was ordering Orchard Thieves, well, I'd go . . . . 'scuse, yup, yup, pint of Heineken, pint of Orchard Thieves. Thanks, yeah.

I turn my body and see that you have in fact ordered and the barman is nodding and already in the process of pulling our pints.

I laugh.

—You're welcome.

—Well thank you but that was totally unnecessary, I'm very capable of ordering my own drink.

—I have no doubt but you see the thing is . . .

You lower your face to mine

—I didn't just want to order for you, I wanted to buy you a drink.

—I'm plenty capable of that too you know.

You stand up and observe me, then you smile.

—I know, I know, but you see now, I've put the ball in your court, now the next round is on you.

The barman places our two pints on the counter.

I pick up my glass and smile.

—You know I'm from Kilkenny, right? You should be careful where you put that ball, we have a tendency to hit them over the bar.

—Did you just turn a tennis reference into a hurling reference?

I scrunch my nose in feigned confusion then clink my glass against yours and head back to Laura and Sam.

I sit down and when I turn around, I see you. You smile in my direction, lift your Waterford jersey to your mouth and kiss it, then you wink at me.

—*Invest in a jersey yet?*

—*Well, I'd probably get more wear out of it than you will with your Waterford one.*

—*Wear it to our first date.*

—*Our first what now?*

I wasn't expecting you to text. I wasn't expecting anything. I was used to one-night stands. I had the art of the one-night stand down to a tee, I got up and I got out. And that's exactly what I was trying to do when I woke up in your Airbnb the morning after we met in Quinns. I slipped

43

out of bed and was picking up my dress from the floor when you woke.

—Where you going?

I stop my careful and quiet movements and turn around.

—Um, home?

You push yourself onto your elbows.

—Already? Don't you want breakfast or like coffee, or something?

I stand up, pulling my dress over my head.

—Aren't all your friends staying here?

You look at me and laugh.

—Yeah, so?

—So, I don't really fancy having breakfast with half the Waterford Intermediates, thanks.

—You really know nothing about GAA do you? The Waterford Intermediates?

You laugh and I roll my eyes.

—Then we'll go out. You can show me some nice breakfast place?

I sit on the side of the bed and attempt to pull on my boots.

—Unless, well, unless I've got this all wrong?

You place your hand on my back and move the strap of my dress off my shoulder, you move towards me and start to kiss my neck. I turn to look at you.

—What do you mean?

—Well, it's starting to look like maybe this was a one-night thing for you.

I shake my hungover head.

—I've no idea what this is.

You pull me back onto the bed before I'm able to get my boots on. You place a palm against my cheek and I do my best to avoid eye contact. Getting up and getting out would have been so much easier.

—What do you want it to be?

I laugh and you look confused, and I want to say aloud that I've never been asked what I wanted before. Instead I say

—I want coffee.

You kiss me then, and it's soft and it's slow.

—Okay then, let's go get coffee.

The next day you text.

—Invested in a jersey yet?

And I accidentally, almost unconsciously, smile at my phone.

It was first-date nerves. It was a sample bottle of Tom Ford from the beauty counter in Brown Thomas. It was perspiration through a white short-sleeved dress. It was rum and tequila and a salt-rimmed glass. It was the underlying fear of being too drunk or too sober. It was normal. It was first-date nerves.

And you were normal. I'd received no unsolicited dick pics. I knew about your family: two brothers, older; a sister, younger. But I didn't know any unnecessary family scandal. You hadn't unloaded your childhood trauma on me, unlike the men I'd met on the apps, the men who used women they met online like some free therapist. You showed vulnerability, but the right amount for someone I'd just met, someone I'd drunkenly slept with once, someone who'd seen the morning-after version of me and still liked me. You'd sent flirty texts and you were cheeky, but it all felt okay. It all felt healthy. It was like suddenly I'd met an adult, someone to talk to, someone to date. And I was ready, hair washed, legs shaved, eyeliner perfected and first-date nerves, the right amount.

I sent a message into the group chat 'Faculty', a chat that consisted of me, Mikala, the new Geography teacher, and Megan, the Art sub. I'd been teaching at St Anne's for three months now and my new teacher friends also felt like a healthy step up from my college buddies. I was happy to leave the past in the past. We'd called the chat 'Faculty' as a piss-take of Principal Morgan's consistent use of the word in every school meeting.

—As facuuuulty members, my expectations are . . .

—You see the facuuuuulty thinks . . .

My message is short and to the point.

—*On way. Skirt too short. Fuck it.*

The responses are immediate and in the form of encouraging GIFs. I drop my phone into my bag and push the door of l'Gueuleton open. You stand up as I walk towards you and you look ridiculously cute in that blue button-down. It quickly becomes a favourite of mine and I will always associate it with this, our first official date.

—I took the liberty of ordering you a drink. I hope that's okay?

I kiss you on the cheek, feeling suddenly very French about the whole evening, and I sit down, pulling my skirt for dignity.

—You look beautiful by the way.

I push my hair behind my ears, so pleased you didn't call me gorgeous.

—Oh I see, toxic masculinity.

You look at me across the table, wide-eyed.

—Ordering my drink for me.

I point at the espresso Martini that sits in front of me, two coffee beans straddling the white foam.

—I'm joking! Jesus.

You shake your head and laugh.

—Don't they do jokes in Waterford? Or is your hurling team the only joke down there?

I lift the cocktail to my lips and sip. And it's strange because I don't have the urge to down it and order a double vodka, which is my usual go-to date routine.

—Seriously now, we have established that the only thing you know about hurling, and I'm going to go out on a limb here – some might even accuse me of going out on a toxic masculine limb – but I'm going to say, the only thing you know about hurling, or indeed any sport, is in fact the name?

I'm smiling as you speak, watching the softness of your face, the ease of your lips as they move.

—Okay, okay. I'll drop the sports stuff.

You hold up your glass (also an espresso Martini).

—I'll cheers to that. So, I know sports aren't your thing, but I want to know what is. Apart from espresso Martinis and Quinns after an All-Ireland.

—Did I mention espresso Martinis that night?

—You did. For quite some time in fact. You had a whole rant about how they are undervalued as an alcoholic beverage and are unfairly considered a 'basic bitch' drink but in fact you feel they are far more nuanced than that. It was quite an in-depth rant in fact and it made me want to hear, well, you know . . .

47

I look at you. Your eyes are green, I hadn't noticed that before and you've got a faint scar above your left eyebrow. Your eyelids are heavy, hooded and the skin underneath is thin and grey.

—No? Tell me?

—Well, it made me want to hear you talk about anything, everything. It made me want to listen to you, just hear you talking about things you love.

You take a long drink from your coupe and the chocolate-coloured liquid is almost completely drained. You look embarrassed, like you've said too much.

—Well, wait until you hear my opinion on IPAs then.

DAVE

I'm screaming and crying, and the screams and the cries are hot in my ears and on my face and I can feel the pain in my forehead and it's burning and bubbling and my hands are shaking. I can't hear what Dave is saying above the noise of my own brain. You know, when you cry so hard you feel the thumping inside you. But he's sorry, I think. He's apologising, I think.

We're in his car at the entrance to Walsh's dad's farm. It's quiet here at this time of night and this is where we come to park; to sit and talk and plan our future, before he drops me home. Our future is bright, mostly, until I get into one of my mad rages of jealousy and go off at him. But then why wouldn't I? There was always another girl, always interrupting our calm.

—Listen. Just listen to me.

Dave is turning my body with his hands, fingers digging into my shoulders as he twists me around in the passenger seat to look at him.

—I'll block her, okay?

I stop crying for a moment but the aftershocks are there and my breath heaves in and out.

—I don't want you to block her.

—Well, *I* want to block her, okay?

It's not okay but I nod my head. He takes out his phone and starts scrolling through his contacts. What I actually want to do is take his phone from his hand and throw it out the window, then start the car and drive over it, feel it crush into tiny pieces under the tyres of his stupid Ford Fiesta.

We were toxic. Isn't that the word that everyone loves to use so much now? Well, we were toxic at the tender age of eighteen – toxic before it became fashionable to be toxic.

We were never alone, there was always someone else interfering. That guy from my English class with the messy hair or the girl he'd met at Irish college. Then there was Walsh's girlfriend, the one who gave me a tampon that night I liked her, trusted her, but she had all those friends who came round and drank vodka and ruffled Dave's hair. My friends didn't like him, and his friends hated me. Maybe that was a sign, maybe that was reason enough for us to go our separate ways. But we didn't. We stuck it out and weathered the storm. I was always storming off and he would delete my number and then he'd show up at my dorm and I'd cry and he'd hold me. Maybe we were addicted to it all, the drama. Or maybe we just didn't know anything else.

We met in Coolfarnamanagh, a few months after the incident with Johnny and Lar. It was summer and I had just finished first year in college. I hadn't spoken to a boy since the accident, could barely think about it. I still hadn't told anyone about my relationship with Lar and it was a secret that ate at me. There was a hole there for sure, a hole that was massive and gaping. A gaping, holey soul; what a thing.

Lar's death changed me. It made me anxious, kept me awake at night. It kept the nightmares coming, visions of his decaying flesh eaten away by maggots. I imagined the crash, the car buckled by the ditch, Johnny's broken neck flopping to one side and Lar's eyes wide as they cut him from his seat, staring at his brother, knowing he was next. I imagined the blood that must have dried around his face, flaked off as they tried to resuscitate him in the hospital, imagined all the thoughts that went through his head. Had he been scared? Had he known that his life was about to end? Had he thought of me?

Everyone thought I was mourning Johnny, and I was too, I guess. But they must have thought it strange that I stayed in bed all weekend and didn't wear make-up any more and didn't shower so much, all because of a guy I'd been on a handful of dates with. Sheila Ryan disappeared. Probably back to Cork, but we never saw her again, not until years later, she didn't like coming home.

We were all affected I suppose, us young people. Such a thing to happen in our small town. Such a thing to happen to me after the death of my sister. And when I got into the car beside my mother because she wanted to take me shopping, wanted to cheer me up, I looked at her hands on the steering wheel, looked at her long fingers and imagined them smashed to pieces on impact, pushed back against her face, hand going through her cheek. Because that's what they'd said, when they'd brought him to the hospital, his hand had gone through his face. And maybe that was a rumour, a tale that came to life after too many pints in O'Donovan's but nonetheless, the image was imprinted on my mind.

Eventually I went out, Lorraine suggested it and the idea was encouraged by my mother. I got dressed and did my hair and I felt human for the first time in a long time.

We went to O'Donovan's and Lorraine was awkward, kept asking if I was okay, looking around and wondering if anything would trigger me, if anything would make me think of young

Johnny Casey. It did, everything did. The bar, the stools, the smell of piss coming out of the men's toilets. This was where we'd met, where we'd first kissed, where I'd watched Johnny's eyes search the bar for Sheila Ryan.

Surprisingly the bar didn't make me think of Lar. It didn't remind me of Lar but when we went out back to find Cian, it hit me, and I could feel Lar's hands under my skirt, rubbing the top of my thigh and his hands were cold now, the cold, lifeless hands of a corpse.

Cian must have seen the look on my face or the colour drain out of it because he passed me a cigarette and I took it. Lorraine had never approved of my new-found hobby but tonight she said nothing and just gave me a half-hearted smile as I sucked the Marlboro and sighed.

—It's quiet out.

She was right, it was.

—No talent at all, except one or two of those lads from Kilmont.

Cian jabbed his cigarette in the direction of a group of lads who stood at the back of the smoking area.

—No sign of Tom?

he asked.

Lorraine shook her head.

—To be honest, I'm done with him.

We nodded and I touched Lorraine's hand gently. The truth was, Tom Doyle was done with her and we all knew it. The signs had been there, he was using her and none of us had said it.

We were back sitting in our usual place when the group from Kilmont came inside. They walked past us laughing and pushing each other in that childish, boyish way that always annoyed me.

Lorraine rolled her eyes.

—Not so sure where you saw the 'talent' there Cian.

Later at the bar, I order a round and the barman is a small spotty guy who's someone's brother. He's the guy who Johnny had signalled, the guy who brought the glass of water to Lar the night he'd gotten into the row. He's the guy who'd come out to get a keg one night when Lar was kissing my neck and we'd had to slide into the shadows, pray he wouldn't see us. And I'd laughed quietly, and Lar had held his hand over my mouth and I'd kissed his palm and he'd whispered

—You're some rogue.

Suddenly I feel someone next to me.

—What's funny?

I look up and I see one of the boys from Kilmont. He's leaning on the bar, elbows resting on a beer spillage.

—You're getting wet there,

I reply.

He smiles and it's a nice smile. It's no Lar but it's nice and he smells nice too and he extends his hand and says

—I'm Dave.

And I reply and I smile too, and it's a nice smile and I say

—Charlotte.

And we shake hands and I feel his warmth and his skin and his fingers and it's only a second and then I'm taking my drinks and I'm walking away as he pats his wet elbow and in just three weeks his hands and his skin and his fingers will be exploring my body, every inch, in the back of his Ford Fiesta, down the lane by Walsh's dad's farm. But I was determined not to let him go all the way in that car.

SAOIRSE

When Saoirse was dating Mikey, she started to sing in the shower and showered twice a day. Her room was cloudy with hairsprays and perfumes and she would spin in her towel, wet hair sticking to her face. I'd sit on the bottom of her bed and watch as she primed herself in front of the mirror.

—Vitamin C to help prevent pigmentation Char.

She applied serums to her face and she was so beautiful in those moments, an array of bottles by her feet.

—Oh Char, when I get my artistry qualification I will be make-up artist to the stars. Can you imagine? Me? Doing make-up for like Gwen Stefani or someone?

I twist the bottle of serum in my hands.

—Would you do movie stars too?

—Oh God yeah. I might do an add-on, special effects make-up. Make people look like monsters or zombies.

She starts to prance around the room, arms out making zombie sounds. Her towel falls.

—Stop looking at me you pervert.

She pulls the towel back up and I laugh.

—Not a lot to perve on really Saoirse.

She laughs and joins me on the bed, resting her head on my shoulder, hair wetting my t-shirt.

—Will you miss me?

I ask it quietly.

—Ah yeah, course I will. You're a pain in the arse, but you know, you're my pain in the arse and I suppose, despite that, I love you.

The night she lost her virginity she came home drunk and knocked on my window.

—Char. Wake up. Char.

I woke bleary-eyed and opened my window and helped her scramble in.

—Thought you were staying at Sinead's place?

She fell onto the bed and threw her arms above her head.

—That's what I told Mum. And, Charlooooootey. Don't tell.

She brings her finger to her lips.

—I won't. But like, what happened?

She sits up and looks at me wide-eyed.

—I am, officially, a woman!

—You didn't?

—I did. And it was glorious. I mean painful and awful but also, glorious. We did it in the back of Tiernan's car.

I grimace.

—A car? You lost your . . . you know . . . in a car?

She rolls over and I can tell she's about to fall asleep.

—Yeah, well the Ritz was booked up Char.

I crawl into bed beside her.

—And he didn't want you to stay and like . . . cuddle?

—In the back of a Prius? No Char, he did not. Besides, I can cuddle you now instead.

I was determined not to lose my virginity in a Prius or in any other car for that matter, so I made sure we planned it perfectly. We waited until Dave's parents were away on holiday and Dave took me out to dinner. I spent hours before the date priming myself in the good mirror. I rummaged in a small Perspex box that was hidden under my bed and pulled out a Juicy Tube. The top was loose and gloss had coagulated around its neck. I rubbed it with my thumb and twisted the tube open. Lightly coloured pink gloss seeped onto my fingers, and I sat up in front of the mirror once more. I started to apply the gloss to my lips, hearing Saoirse's words in my ear.

—It's the Bridget Jones conundrum.

I'd looked at her, confused.

—The what?

—Jesus Charlotte, your popular culture knowledge is actually embarrassing. It's like . . .

She placed her lipstick on the bathroom sink and turned to look at me, perched on the edge of the bath watching her get ready.

—So Bridget Jones is going on a date and she wants to look good so she thinks about wearing those knickers that like, hold you in. But then she's like, if she gets lucky and he comes home with her he's going to see the pants and that's so unsexy.

—Right?

—Right, so the conundrum is, wear the pants so you look hot and get lucky but then you're wearing ugly pants . . . or, wear sexy pants but then you don't look as hot so he doesn't even see them.

—What does she do?

—She wears the ugly pants.

Saoirse turns back around and picks up her lipstick.

—So my Bridget Jones conundrum is . . . wear the sexy red lipstick but then if I pull it's all over the guy's face, but if I don't wear it, I'm not as sexy so I won't pull.

She sighs and puts the lipstick back down.

—But luckily . . .

She turns to look at me, deepening her voice and holding a tube of lipgloss above her head.

—On the third day God created Juicy Tubes! Sexy lips, no transfer, kiss as many boys as you like.

I sit back and look at myself – the gloss is very early noughties but Dave won't have a clue, he'll be too excited to get me home.

Dave takes me to a fancy Italian and orders wine, a full bottle and we share it, feeling like proper adults. Dave holds my hand across the table and orders us a taxi home and when we lie together, I feel safe, connected. It doesn't hurt as much as I imagined, but it doesn't feel particularly good either, but Dave holds me and we fall asleep together like that. The next morning, I think about Saoirse and the Prius and I wish that she had had a different experience, something comparable to mine, maybe that would have made all the difference. I also think about what she'd said.

—I am, officially, a woman!

I looked at myself in Dave's bathroom mirror. She'd been right about the lipstick, there was nothing smeared across my face but somehow I couldn't relate to the rest, I certainly didn't feel like a woman. I didn't feel anything at all.

There were moments when it all made sense. Mornings that were rich with love and longing, sleep clouding our eyes, resting on our pillows. And Dave would turn to me in those moments, reach for me with his desire and cradle me in his embrace. I was happy and I was safe and the day opened around us and our bodies were raw and yearning.

The bed was small in my university halls dwelling and we shared it, Dave's body heating mine and mine his, so in the middle of the night I would reach out for the wall and place my bare back against it to cool my skin. He held both of my hands, séance-like, and I'd smiled and it didn't hurt and we lay together afterwards and stared at my ceiling and he said

—Are you okay?

And of course, I was.

There was always a sense of security with Dave and maybe that's why we stayed together so long. I always felt safe. I felt safe when I got my morning text, when he told me about Kilmont and the roof he was working on and his father and the new dog and what the boys had said at poker the other night. I felt safe when I got off the bus and he was there to collect me and when he touched my knee on the way home.

I felt safe when he came to Dublin, when he stood there in Heuston station with his hurling bag on his shoulder and I felt safe when he kissed my neck and my back and peeled away my clothes and held me there, naked against him, skin on skin.

But the memories aren't all good. You have to be careful with that. The good memories always try to outshine the bad ones and our minds can play tricks on us. Because even though I felt safe with Dave, something was wrong, something was very wrong.

I called him my first love because what was Lar only a pipe dream or a secret and it felt good to say it, to Lorraine and to Cian and to Pauline, my housemate. And Pauline would shift uneasily in her chair, glass of wine held tightly between two palms and she'd smile but I knew she hated him.

And that was a sign. Your friends want the best for you. Mostly. Unless you've got some jealous friend and that's what Dave would say.

—She's jealous Char, she doesn't have anyone, she's lonely.

And I listened because I liked him, and I liked the smell of his cologne and the feel of his lips and I liked the sex and the security of it, and I couldn't imagine doing that with someone else.

—He's controlling.

Pauline would look at me disapprovingly and drop her empty glass into the sink and go to bed. And I'd sit up in our kitchen and look at my phone and see Dave's text and smile and feel sick at the same time. Because maybe I wasn't seeing it. Maybe I was missing something.

We spent every weekend together. I'd go to Kilmont or he'd get the train to me. And we didn't go out or see friends, we just stayed in with each other, locked in our own little world. And he'd trace his fingers along my jaw and I'd massage his back. And we'd hold hands and walk in the park and drink cheap wine and pretend that we were grown-ups. And as time passed I thought less of Lar. Less of his body, buckled in his Renault Megane, less of his cold, papery skin in the coffin. I thought less of Johnny too and his big eyes and his tanned arms. Because now I had Dave. And Dave was all I needed.

Every night he'd ring me and Pauline would roll her eyes as I left whatever party we were at to take the call. And I'd stand on the balcony, or by the toilets or outside the door and I'd talk to him. And he spoke about how the Kilkenny Intermediates were doing while I tried to explain Modernism or the definition of self and he'd call me a posh wanker, up there with all my smart Dublin friends and I'd laugh because it was a joke. I always thought that it was a joke. And then I invited him to the class ball and I bought him that nice suit and we stood in my room and I applied red lipstick to my mouth and he was sitting on my bed. And I turned to him and I looked at him and he sort of grimaced and I looked confused. And he smiled and reached over and pulled a tissue from its box. And he stood up slowly then and he approached me and placed the tissue against my mouth and he rubbed my lips. Then he threw the tissue into the bin and went to the bathroom. And I lifted my hand-held mirror and I looked at my reflection and the redness that was smeared onto my cheeks. And I looked at my reflection and the half woman that stared back at me.

I imagined Saoirse's face then, when she'd come home after her dates, the faint stain of rouge on her chin, her face scrunched up and giggling as she told me all about boys and kissing and what

I would one day experience. I thought about the delicacy with which she spoke of boys and their flirtations, the great feeling of falling in love and being swooned. I wondered if she always felt that way, if men had always been like this with her, sweet and delicate and kind. Of course, I knew, they hadn't.

Dave didn't have the best family life and I'd tell people that, like an excuse. His father was rough, not abusive in the usual sense, didn't hit him or anything like that but he was rough. He was old-fashioned and Dave told people that, like an excuse. And Dave's father didn't like me and he made that clear. I had notions, I went to university in Dublin and I looked down on people like him, people who stayed in Kilmont or Coolfarnamanagh all their lives. Except of course I didn't, but there are some points not worth stressing.

Dave's dad worked hard. He worked around the clock and he held that work and that sacrifice for his family like a trophy. But the trophy soon became a weapon and the pride a manipulation and you could tell he resented it. Resented the life he'd worked so hard to give his sons. Dave had two younger brothers and they were wild, wilder than Dave and they resisted their father more. I always felt that Dave sat somewhere in the middle, trying to please his father, trying to please his brothers and somehow falling short of both.

And I felt it. I felt it when he picked me up from the bus on Friday evenings. As we drove down the uneven lanes to his house, as we stood in his porch and kissed before going inside. There was always an atmosphere in that house, an atmosphere that was hidden beneath the loud noise of his brothers playing computer games or the whirring of the washing machine in the kitchen. There was an atmosphere that hung in the air and drifted through the brief moments of silence. And I'd sit on his single bed, with the striped duvet cover that had piled in the laundry and I'd look at the dartboard on his wall and I'd watch him close his bedroom door quietly. Then he'd turn to me and I'd see relief on his face, relief that we'd made it inside secretly and didn't have to speak to his dad or disturb his brothers.

And those moments were special because that's when Dave was at his most vulnerable, here in his home, where his mother had hanged herself from the shower curtain in the bathroom. And the curtain had since been ripped down but the tiny rings still hung around the bar and rattled in the breeze when the window was open and I always wondered why nobody had taken them down too. Here, Dave was quiet and Dave was gentle and I felt his body and I felt him dissolve into me. And there was something else, something besides the vulnerability and the quietness, there was something else that I felt in Dave during these moments. And he would hold me on his single bed and he would try so hard to appear manly but the room was too small, the dartboard too boyish and the paint on the wall too blue and his eyes were filled with a sadness. And I wanted to hold him then, hold him still as he moved on top of me, and caress his face and his cheeks and tell him it was all okay, it would all be okay. But I didn't, because I didn't know how he'd react and I let him come inside me because I was on the pill and I let him smile and lie down beside me and we'd look out the window at the night as it fell around us. And later we'd leave the house quietly again and he'd drop me home.

*

To this day I can't really say that he was controlling. I mean, he was. But so was I in my own way. We were enmeshed, a word Saoirse had taught me when I was seven and didn't understand, a word I still don't really understand now. Our days were in sync and we always knew what the other was doing. I knew what Dave had for breakfast, he knew where I went for lunch and nights were filled with long phone calls that kept us awake into the darkness.

It was, I suppose, too much, but it felt normal, it felt right. I wanted to hear from him first thing and he wanted to be the last person I spoke to at night. But it became difficult when I discovered red wine and late nights in the common room, and stories about literary erotica. My friends in Dublin weren't like Dave and they weren't like Lorraine or Cian either and the two lives, Coolfarnamanagh and Dublin, seemed so separate to me now. But I loved Dave, I think. I certainly thought I did at the time and so I always called him when I got home and some nights I'd be drunk and talking about something stupid like Freud's theory on blow jobs and I'd hear the annoyance in his voice.

Then he started going out, midweek, with the lads. And he had new friends and they had girlfriends and their girlfriends had sisters. And in my mind, all these sisters looked like Sheila Ryan and I was jealous of them all.

—Ugh, it's so obvious, he's jealous Charlotte.

And Pauline was right because Dave did have a terrible jealous streak but then so did I. And I hated when he went out during the week even though I was out as well and I'd sit in the corner of the bar, or the pub or the room of whoever's flat we were in and I'd stare at my screen and I'd wait for him to text.

And he always did, but the waiting killed me and a knot would form in my stomach when hours went by with nothing and I imagined him with some Sheila Ryan lookalike up against his Ford Fiesta and Pauline would touch my knee and say

—Hun, you alright?

And I think she knew, or at least she knew something. Maybe she thought I was upset or traumatised by what she later called the 'abuse'. But I'd just smile and nod and say

—Yeah, yeah, grand

and slip my phone back into my pocket and pray for it to vibrate.

So I was as bad as him, you could say, but I was in love and isn't there a quote about how everyone is a fool in love? So what I was feeling was natural then. And I didn't want it to end, I couldn't lose someone, not again, so I clung to this thing, this fluid thing that seemed so intangible and it wasn't until years later that I realised, all connections are.

I could always smell Dave, after. I could smell him on my bed, on the pillow, on my sheets and on my hands. The faint scent of his cologne or his sweat or just his essence. It was a smell I hoped would linger. There was the smell of sex in the morning that hung on the air and we would never get up to open a window, we basked in it. And we lay beside one another, naked and warm and we loved it and we smiled in it. And we stayed unclothed all weekend and I would only pull on his t-shirt if I had to go to the kitchen to get us water and even then I had the look of sex about me. It was in my hair, tangled and messy, on my cheeks, flushed and warm, it was on my lips, a wide grin, and Pauline always knew, never came knocking, never asked could she come in, so we never needed to crack the window, let the fresh air in to cleanse us.

I didn't shower when Dave went home on Sunday evenings, back down to Kilmont, I held on to the feeling of him on my skin. It was not until Monday morning that I'd wash the weekend away, let soap lather on my skin and watch as the memory of Dave circled the plughole and disappeared. Then I'd change the sheets, put on a bra for the first time in two days. I'd stand in the mirror those mornings and look at myself, my slender thighs, the small swell of my belly, my breasts that sat high on my chest. I'd rub my hand along my body, the parts I wished to be more toned, more tight. I'd run my fingers over my nipples and up along my neck, touch the light marks left there by Dave's mouth. Then I'd get dressed, pull a scarf around my neck and my shoulders bitten and branded in a moment of passion.

It never really felt like he was gone because we spoke so much and blessed be the powers of technology because it wasn't long before there were multiple platforms for us to communicate on. And we used them all, the WhatsApps and the Instagrams and the Snapchats and with each new way of communication came a stream of new anxieties. There were blue ticks that signalled he'd read my message, grey ticks that meant he hadn't, unopened Snapchats but a Snapchat score that indicated he'd opened others. There were likes on Instagram photos by other girls, friend requests on Facebook and there was the endless questioning and vibration of my brain as I tried to keep up with it all. Of course there were no answers, only shrugs and opinions and often the opinion was that you just had to trust your significant other these days. But trust was something that did not come naturally to me, does not come naturally to me. So I found myself watching his story at 2 a.m. to see if the background was his or in fact the bedroom of some girl he was seeing on the sly. I became obsessed and it probably showed. It showed in the dark circles that sat beneath my eyes, it showed in the poor sentence structure of my essays and it showed in my distraction as I sat in pubs with my friends trying to live this Dublin life.

I felt like I kept the paranoia to myself, kept the questions burning like acid in my throat, like the heartburn of a pregnant woman. But maybe it was obvious in what I said and how I said it. Maybe he knew that I was drowning in this worry. The distance wasn't great, Dublin to Kilmont was a short commute but still it felt too far. At night I'd pace the floor, watching my phone sit silently on the bedside table and when it vibrated I'd feel a sense of calm come over me and I'd laugh at myself and the worry that had held me so tightly in its grasp minutes before. And in my defence, he wasn't much better and if I was slow to reply or didn't text him first thing in the morning, there would always be a phone call making sure that I was okay.

—It's really not normal, you need to give each other space.

But what did Pauline know? She was single, like Dave said, single and had never been in love. But some of our friends weren't single and I watched them because I wanted to know if this was normal, but I couldn't compare. My friend Shona lived with her boyfriend's family so of course she could come on nights out and leave her phone on silent and not look at it until we were in the queue in McDonald's and she was asking him to come pick her up. And Miriam was with her boyfriend for four years so she knew every girl he'd ever dated, which was very few and anyway he wasn't very good-looking so got little attention. But Dave and I were different. Dave had a history with the girls of Kilmont, he'd slept with four other people whereas I had lost my virginity to him. To him, sleeping with another person was old hat but for me it would take serious thought and consideration. And honestly, I couldn't even try to imagine it. So I never really found out if it was normal, normal that he'd accuse me of cheating if I stayed in Dublin for the weekend to study, normal if I suspected he was cheating because he used a different cologne, normal for him to appear at my dorm as a surprise on a Wednesday night and plead with me not to go to the social that Pauline had spent weeks organising.

—Are you actually fucking kidding me right now?

I look at Pauline, eyes wide, arms akimbo at her hips.

—Are you fucking kidding?

she repeats.

—What am I meant to do, he's sitting right in there. I didn't know he was coming. It was a surprise.

She looks at me as I point at the door to my bedroom. We are both standing in the hallway and she lies back against her own door rolling her eyes. She crosses her arms sharply at her stomach.

—It isn't a surprise. What part of that don't you get?

I look at her, lips parted, tongue held to the side between her teeth.

—He literally doesn't want you to go.

—He does, he's told me to go actually but like, I can't leave him here, on his own, how mean is that?

She breathes out heavily, knowing that it's a lie, knowing that Dave would never tell me to go out without him.

—You know what else is mean Char? Not coming to my social. Not coming to support your supposed best friend when she organises an event and is fucking shitting herself at the thought of it.

—Well, maybe I could bring him. Are there any tickets left?

Pauline turns around and goes into her room, she lets the door slap shut behind her. I wait outside. I can hear the murmur of Dave playing a video on his phone in my room, I can hear him laughing. I'm hoping, praying that there are no tickets left. Pauline comes back out carrying her laptop.

—No Char, of course there are no tickets left. As you know, I have been promoting the fuck out of this event for weeks now – as you know, and as fucking 'wet-the-bed' inside knows and is the precise reason he is up here tonight.

She always referred to Dave as wet-the-bed, her term for men who were effeminate but straight. I let out an inner sigh of relief but bite my lower lip to show disappointment. I want to go to the social, I want to support Pauline but I do not want Dave mixing with my college friends and passing comments and judgements on them, starting rows with guys who come over and hug me.

—Buuut, considering I organised the whole fucking thing.

She looks at the laptop screen balanced in one hand and she hits a few keys with the other.

—I can get him in.

—What?

—I can get him in. Your excuse of a boyfriend will go to the ball. But you owe me Charlotte, I swear to fucking God.

—But he has nothing to wear and—

my protest is cut short by Pauline's glare.

—Cinderella can wear what the fuck he likes, I've a taxi coming in ten minutes and I better see both of you out there waiting for it.

Dave had this mole on his shoulder that I was sure would kill him. And I'd look at it, as he lay in the bed next to me, my single bed, my back pressed against the wall to cool me. And I'd trace my finger over it and try to memorise the shape and the contours so I'd know if it changed, know if it were malignant, a melanoma come to take my Dave away. He didn't go to the doctor, as a rule. Like his father, he thought it was a waste of money and the Earth would cure you, and if it was your time to go, it was your time to go. But when he got a cold he'd hunch in front of the TV and I'd bring him Lemsip and he was like a child then and didn't seem to mind my nursing.

When the summer came after our first year together, we celebrated our anniversary, celebrated meeting in O'Donovan's twelve months before and now the pub was a reminder of me and Dave, the memory of Lar almost erased. I spent most of that summer in Dave's house and I'd lie on his single bed when he went to work, tell my mother I was at Lorraine's, not because she'd mind, just because I was embarrassed. Staying at a boy's house meant sex and I didn't need the constant interrogation.

—Does your dad not mind me staying here so much?

Dave shrugged and I couldn't tell if that meant he didn't know how his father felt or if he didn't care.

Some mornings I'd meet his father in the kitchen and he'd look at me with that deep, penetrative stare and he'd say something like

—Oh you finally got up.

Or

—Isn't it well for some to have nothing to do?

And I hated him, more with each passing day, each sly comment. But I ignored him because Dave told me it was the only thing to do.

—Pay no heed.

But as June rolled into July and the sun sat higher and the days got warmer, so too did Dave's father seem to warm to me. He stopped passing comments and started saying hello and he seemed, now, less scary, less awful. So one morning when making coffee I said

—Would you like one?

And he nodded and I poured the coffee and I handed him the cup and then the milk and he looked at me and for the first time it was without that awful stare. And it meant nothing, just a gesture, just a way of being kind but he took it the wrong way and later that day with Dave still at work, he came into the bedroom and he sat on Dave's bed and he reached out and touched my breasts over my top. And when I jumped back and pulled my hands across my chest he got up and he went to the door then he turned around and he called me a slut.

It was weeks before I told Dave. I made excuses not to visit the house but in the end it became too obvious that something was up. Dave's dad was off visiting their granny in Tipperary when I said I'd come over and we sat on Dave's bed and I cried and I told him the story.

He was quiet then and he looked at me and his face was motionless, cold and then he put his arm around me and he held me and I felt safe again, safe to be with Dave, safe to be in this house once more. But later, he took me by the hand and into the bath and we stood in it, even in the absence of the curtains and as I washed the shampoo out of my hair he grabbed my body, pulled me back to him and bent me over. And he put himself inside me then and gripped my hair and he pushed me hard up against the damp wall. And it was rough, rougher than usual and it hurt and I cried out as he came and he cried out too and he said

—You're a slut, you're a fucking slut.

And maybe I was.

And later that night I traced my fingers along the mole and I checked that it hadn't changed and I felt a slight disappointment. And I felt bad about that feeling, felt guilty. But when it was his time, it would be his time. And as it turned out, his time was pretty near and three weeks after he fucked me in his bathtub, he was found, one end of a scarf tied to the shower curtain rings, the ones that were attached to the curtain his mother had used to kill herself with, and the other end around his neck.

And there was Dave, swinging, naked from the waist down.

YOU

You weren't fond of Dublin, said the only reason you came every weekend was to see me. I never imagined I would convince you to move. I never imagined I could have that power. Before me, you came to Dublin maybe once a year. Our meeting had been chance. You called it fate. I laughed and jokingly called it bad luck. You were almost finished with the apprenticeship when we met. An electrician, just like your dad and your dad's dad.

—I suppose I'm boring and predictable to you.

You're standing in my room, running your fingers along the books that line my overstocked bookshelf. I'm lying on my bed, and I sit up now and reach for your waist, pulling you closer. I start to undo your belt as you pick up a copy of *Dubliners*.

—I've never read Joyce.

I pull your belt loose from the constraints of your trouser loops and the buckle lands loudly on the wooden floor.

—I don't know if I fit into this life, Miss Murphy.

I pull your zipper down and your jeans loosen. You're still holding the book, turning it over in your hands. I tug your jeans down and your boxers move with them.

—I don't know if I can compete with these posh families you're teaching and these after-curricular classes where you sit around and talk about Dante.

Your cock is hard and it slips out over your elasticated waistband like it's searching for my mouth. I put my lips around you. You let out a low moan.

—I don't know if . . .

I move my mouth over you slowly.

—Fuck.

You drop the book. Joyce falls to the floor beside your belt.

I take my mouth away and look up at you.

—Fuck Dante, I say.

You nod at me in agreement.

Those weekend mornings. I imagine them now. The sun creeping in through thin curtains and dancing across the uneven skin on your face. The white mark of the scar above your eyebrow glimmering in the light. Your eyelids are closed lightly and you look peaceful. Your eyelashes resting on your upper cheek move faintly in your slumber and they remind me of spiders' legs, threading daintily.

Your chest moves up and down with your breath and it lifts the duvet slightly. I move under your arm and smell your skin, feel your warmth on my face as it half sticks to you. We are engulfed by morning now and the sheets are heavy with sleep, dead weights on my legs and feet. I move my hand across your stomach daring to wake you and I feel you move. Your body is soft and you manoeuvre it towards me. I take you in my arms and your head nestles into me. I stroke your head, your hair flattened by night and your lips waken, opening on my neck. You taste me with your mouth, your tongue, and I move my body with you. We slip under the covers then and this is our secret, sacred place.

When you get up to make coffee I relax into your side of the bed. It's always warmer than mine, like your body emits more heat. I like to lie here, where you've slept, feel your memory on my skin.

If I could go back to any moment in our relationship it would be those mornings. Long mornings where I wore your t-shirt and sipped dark coffee while you lay on the floor amongst paper and felt tips.

You spent the mornings drawing me. I would toss my hair and arch my back, make jokes and never stay still so you had to draw me from memory as I stepped over you, bare legs grazing your cheeks as I watered the plants that sat in the window.

You drew me and you drew the streetlights. You drew big oak trees and rivers that ran deep into the valley. You drew other women, women I didn't know, didn't recognise but I never asked who they were. You drew one woman who had a tattoo on her thigh. You drew this carefully and I watched as you etched the tattoo, intricate lines, onto her body. You often spoke about becoming a tattoo artist but you never really tried. You said it would be too difficult, you had to know people, there was no formal training. But when I watched your hands move, the delicacy, the attention to detail and the art that was produced from your fingertips, I knew you could do it.

I lay back and let you draw me. This was our bohemian dream.

KYLE

All of our friends were gone and despite the fact that the club was still full and busy, I felt like we were alone. There was a silence that hung softly between us and it followed us as we moved through the crowd. We walked from bar to dance-floor, I was his shadow and I stayed close to him and it felt, in this moment, as if everyone moved out of our way as we approached, a parting of the sea. Kyle swung his arm back towards me, hand outstretched as we got to the dancefloor but he did not turn his head. I looked down at his pale skin and then I gripped his wrist, I was too afraid to hold his hand, that seemed to me too intimate.

When we got to the centre of the dancefloor, Kyle spun around. He was smiling and moving his body slowly in time to the music. His hair was long then, floppy and he ran his fingers through it. I smiled and started to relax. I joined in the dancing. Kyle laughed at the music and I knew he hated this place, this club. His dancing was ironic, and I would have enjoyed this if I hadn't been so nervous.

Pauline and I had moved in with Kyle only days before and I had no idea how close we would become. He had a girlfriend, Claire, who always wore nude lipstick and smelled like rose and moved languidly from his bedroom to the kitchen and never said much. She visited once or twice a week and they cooked together, stood by the sink splashing sudsy water at one another. She laughed quietly but Kyle's was a guttural laugh and it moved the house, moved me. I would come to the fridge to retrieve my wine and watch as he placed a hand over her eyes and brought a spoon of some concoction to her lips.

—Guess,

he'd say and she'd giggle as she tasted. Then she'd peer through his fingers trying to get a look at what he'd put in her mouth.

It irked me. I wanted to shout, basil or rosemary or whatever I could see, but the game was more complex than that, Kyle had made a sauce or a roux and I was too used to processed condiments to know how to play so instead I'd close the fridge door loudly and bottle swinging from my fingertips I'd head back upstairs, feeling his eyes on me, all the time.

Now I wonder if there was more malice to the game, if he liked to hide her eyes so she couldn't see, couldn't see where he was looking, couldn't see how he looked at me.

He spins around now and throws his palm outwards, gesturing for me to take it and I do. He twists and turns my body to a foreign beat and I know he is making a mockery of this DJ. We look ridiculous but I play along, so easily manipulated by his movements. He grips my fingers in his and his skin feels hot against mine. I feel myself get dizzy but I throw my head back nonetheless, the lights above flashing blue, green and red, the sound from the speaker distorted as my body whips past, his hand the only thing that feels stationary.

Then the music slows, the night is coming to an end. I let go of him and stand still for a minute. I bring my hand to my mouth, feel the Red Bull reflux in my throat, the smell of cigarettes on my fingers. I am motionless for a moment; the lights are still dimmed, the bodies still move around me. Kyle's face is still in front of me. I watch as he checks his phone. Perhaps she's texted him, asked him if he's staying with her tonight. Or maybe it's just a simple text to say she misses him, hopes he's having a good time. But when he lifts his head and his eyes meet mine, once again I think maybe she hasn't texted at all because his eyes look at me differently now, like they did in the kitchen, like I imagined they looked as they burned into my back.

He comes closer to me then, he places his hand on my waist, he brings his mouth to my ear.

—He is the best DJ I have ever heard.

All of a sudden I can't sense if he is being sarcastic or not. All of a sudden it doesn't matter. His breath is warm against my cheek and I don't move. I stay still and I don't respond. He brings his face closer to mine and his lips are inches from my mouth. We stay there, in this moment, a moment I will think about months later when I least expect it. We stay there and we breathe each other's air, see our own reflection in each other's pupils. Then the music stops and the lights come on, drenching us all in a sharp white hue. I blink and when I open my eyes he is gone. In just those few seconds he is gone. I look around and see him beckoning me and I follow once again through the crowd towards the exit, but this time it feels like nobody moves out of our way at all.

*

Maybe I can trace the change in me to Kyle. Maybe it all started with him, if we really think about it. If we really look at the facts, at the patterns, at how everything turned out after him. He broke me in so many ways but then I guess, I was the one who broke him totally, in the end. I do think it was love though, but then, maybe it always is. Maybe I'm always in love but I just choose the wrong men. Kyle was certainly the wrong man.

It started as friendship, as these things often do. Pauline and I moved into a shared house with Kyle after our third-year application for halls was declined. He had advertised the rooms on NetHub because his friends had both moved to France on Erasmus. He seemed nice, normal, fond of a drink but not a total night owl. The friendship between us blossomed easily and soon I was spending all of my time in his bedroom. We seemed to have a lot in common, similar interests in music, dark sense of humour, it drove Pauline mad. When he broke up with his girlfriend, and made sure I was the first to know, the friendship quickly turned into something more.

—No, no, it's embarrassing, stop.

I roll onto my belly and face Kyle's laptop screen as my pixelated face comes into focus.

Welcome back to Uni TV.

It was the second episode of my first-year TV series with the communications society where I interviewed a panel of comedians.

—I'm drunk there, I'm literally pissed. Don't watch that.

But we do, both of us panned out on Kyle's bed, his body, warm and close to mine. We stay up half the night drinking cheap whiskey and watching bizarre videos on YouTube.

—My back aches man.

I offer to massage it and Kyle lies out flat while I straddle his back. I'm drunk and my hands are too heavy.

—Jesus fucking Christ, don't kill me.

I'm laughing and apologising as he twists his body around, but I don't move, sit on top of him, smiling.

—Yeah, don't give up the day job, alright?

I'm still laughing when he pokes my belly. I lean over the side of the bed and he holds my waist as my fingers reach for the neck of the whiskey bottle.

—Another drink sir?

I pour the dark liquid from a height and he opens his mouth. He almost chokes and I throw my head back laughing. He sits up and now his face is close to mine and we sit, interlocked in each other. He doesn't say anything, just takes the bottle from my hand and places it on the floor.

—You're beautiful.

—I know.

I reply with nonchalance but I feel the deep thuds of my heart somewhere in my chest. He brings his face close and places his lips on mine. We sit like this for a moment and I wish we had left it there, wish I hadn't pushed my mouth into his, my lips, my tongue, my heart all forced onto him and mangled and distraught and destroyed. He holds my face and my neck and he pushes me back into his bed, my head against his pillow. He puts his hands up my top and all of a sudden I no longer feel twenty, but like a teenage girl again, like I'm losing my virginity, my mind. His hands move to my jeans and he struggles with the buttons but soon they are undone and he moves his head between my legs. I come fast and I feel embarrassed.

He doesn't look at me as I leave and I feel funny. I'm drunk yes, but that's not it. I fill a glass of water in the kitchen before I go upstairs to my room. It overflows and spills onto my fingers as I open my bedroom door. I see my phone on my bed and I hear it vibrate. It's him.

—*Goodnight x*

I gulp the water too fast and cough it back up on myself. I reply

—*Xx*

I lie down, my chest is wet and everything feels fuzzy, but everything feels fine.

The following night we went to Julia's for a party. There were so many bottles of cheap wine, the smell of smoke in the air and open books, and phones playing music and people sitting cross-legged on the floor drumming beats on their knees, talking shite from their mouths. There were I love yous and I want yous, there were bodies moving closer, skin grazing skin as we all got drunker and there were dark corners where lips touched lips and mixed with the smoke. And then there was me and then then there was Julia and she was leaning on Kyle, elbows resting on his knee. And his eyes were big and wide and she smiled and she tossed her hair over her bare shoulder and she brought her face that had no make-up close to his. And I sat at the other side of the room and I touched my cheek, and I felt the dampness of my foundation and I wanted to scrub it all away.

And I slumped back against the couch as Zach spoke into my ear about masturbation and his breath was sour against my face and I drank the cheap wine from the bottle and I imagined Kyle's hands running down my neck and the warmth of his bedroom in the attic and the quietness of it and how I would climb the stairs every night after twelve and nobody knew, or if they did, nobody said anything, and Kyle would take me from my clothes and he would run his mouth along my naked flesh and afterwards I would creep downstairs and lie in my own bed and look out my window as the moon moved across the sky and fell asleep.

And Julia was laughing now, and her laugh was posh, just like her accent, and her face was posh and her clothes were posh, and she seemed so happy and so comfortable in her own skin. And she was skinny, like really skinny and pale, and her arms were long as they reached out and touched him and I sat with my fake-tanned legs that weren't fat but weren't as skinny as hers, and I saw myself rubbing brown lotion down them outside the shower with a self-tanning mitt, and I thought about the ridiculousness of it and what he must think of me. And at the same time I thought how I only ever judged myself like this through another's eyes, through a man's eyes and I scolded myself as Zach raved on about self-love and then I saw Pauline and her eyes narrowed on Julia's back and her lips moved into a thin line as her stare moved to Kyle, and I knew in that moment that she knew. I knew she had heard me climb the stairs at night, had heard the movements of Kyle's body on top of mine and I knew she hated him in this moment, and I knew she hated me for keeping it a secret.

—Because how can you expect a guy to know how to make you orgasm if you don't even know yourself like?

Zach's voice was really grating now and his emphasis on the 's' in orgasm was making me feel sick and he was just repeating himself and this was a played-out record I had to listen to at every party. Every Trinity Arts night was the same. And suddenly I hated everyone in this room. I hated their voices and their accents and how we were all drunk all of the time, and how we talked about the clitoris and the vagina like we were inventing the wheel and he kept going.

—Like there's no taboo about a guy masturbating.

And again he was emphasising the 's' and Julia was terribly close to Kyle now and his hand was on her shoulder and I knew what that meant and I knew what was happening.

—So why are women not allowed to learn about their clitoris. Clitorisssssssss

And I wanted to scream and say I didn't care about how there was no taboo for men and how they could all go and pull themselves off to death for all I cared because Julia was leaning forward now and she was pressing her mouth to Kyle's and all the unfairness in the world, all the wage gaps and rape culture and slut-shaming and pigeonholing, nothing mattered to me now because Kyle was taking Julia upstairs to his attic room, and he was going to take her from her clothes and run his mouth over her naked flesh, and the only taboo tonight would be me, if I fingered myself in my room beneath the attic to the sound of their aggressive fucking.

I got my first proper job in Brown Thomas when I started second year. I imagined what Saoirse would have said.

—You jammy little bitch. Can you get me discount?

My friends in college were not as excited.

—Ugh, it's like the worst place in the world.

—Ugh capitalism.

—Ugh money.

—Ugh.

But I liked it. Between lectures on popular culture in new media and cans of Druids and conversations about imperialism at after-parties, the four-hour shifts in Brown Thomas were my release. I started on a make-up counter and I'd stand behind it practising my best Saoirse smile. A smile that gave me an approachable edge but also made me feel like I was better than my customers. I had the inside scoop. I was the pro. I knew what was in all the bottles. I knew how to apply them and if you were lucky I would share this wisdom with you. I was no make-up artist, I felt I was just a salesperson, but I watched the artists all day, the way the lightest touch of a brush could transform someone's face. I was mesmerised.

Kyle found the whole thing foolish.

—Why would you like, paint your face? I much prefer natural women.

I'd dig my nails into my palms when he said it, feel my contour start to burn on my face. I usually loved the feeling of foundation as it covered my skin. Loved the smell of newly opened lipstick. Loved the sound of a bottle opening, the feel of the final dust of powder. But somehow, when I was with Kyle, he always managed to make me feel stupid and insecure.

In work I could be a different version of myself. A self that layered colours on my 'canvas'.

I started smoking for a few months, to impress Kyle, and soon became part of the BT crew that smoked at the staff entrance under the 'Smoking Prohibited' sign. That's where it all happened, where you got all the latest goss, who'd cheated on who, who'd abused their discount, who was still swiping for free lunch on a Sunday even though they didn't work here any more. Saoirse would have loved it.

83

My bedroom soon became a junkyard for the little beige and brown bags with the black ribbon. Products I didn't need or use cluttering up my desk and an overdraft I did not want to tell my mother about. It was addictive. It was, in Saoirse's words, life-changing.

I loved the small talk with the smokers. We were not friends, merely acquaintances held together by a large building and a set of ever-changing brand values.

I stand outside the entrance and Mark from Chanel joins me. His face is immaculate, every line or bump disguised by fifty-euro concealer and eyelashes painted with the blackest mascara.

—Lighter?

I pull my lighter from my pocket and pass it to him.

—Do you remember Juicy Tubes?

He drags on his cigarette and passes back the lighter.

—Juicy Tubes? Lancôme did them?

—Yes, and they came in loads of different colours and sets?

—That's the one.

He smokes deeply and waves at two girls across the road, both leaning against the wall of Clarendon Street church, smokes in hand.

—They were class.

I say it smiling and stub my cigarette against the wall.

—Cult classics. When's your break over?

I look at my watch.

—Five minutes.

—Tragic.

I nod and head back inside.

Kyle just didn't get it.

*

There were simple moments that felt like peace. The ease of rolling over in his bed as morning broke around us, Pauline turning on the shower or singing loudly in the kitchen as she made breakfast. Moments when Kyle's smile was pure and he woke slowly, arms around me, chin resting against my neck. These moments were brief, fleeting and soon I was dressed and heading out to class and he was joking with Pauline and they bounced their jokes back and forth across the kitchen table like a game of tennis. And I'd place a friendly kiss on his head and ruffle his hair because we were friends, we were best friends and that was okay and nobody asked anything about it.

But then there were the nights when he didn't reply to my text or told me not to come up to his room. Nights when I heard other women on the stairs, the lilt of an accent, the weight of their footsteps. Nights when I stood against the fridge with a drink in my hand, nights when we dimmed the lights, and our friends came over and Pauline was hosting and I would drink too fast and he flirted with every girl that walked into our apartment. And those nights were not peaceful and I was always pissed, too pissed to make sense of it all, too pissed to express how I felt, too pissed when he took me upstairs and held my body up against the wall. Too pissed to feel the regret and the pain and the hatred. But not too pissed to make him stop, not too pissed that he'd bring me back down to my own room and lay me down and say no Char, not tonight Char and place a kiss there on my forehead. So I'd wake with a banging headache and I'd look at Kyle then, lying beside me sleeping and I'd remember him rubbing his body up against some girl the night before and the look on his face as the girl left and how he came to me then, standing there with my back against the fridge, and how I'd wanted to shout fuck you, and empty my drink over his head and walk away. But instead I'd turned my cheek and felt his palm on my hip and his long fingers pulling at my waistband and minutes later I was bent over in his bedroom and fighting the tears that were threatening as I gripped his bedside table.

But the moments of peace still came, after. No matter how many times I cried, no matter how many times my heart dropped into my stomach, no matter how many girls grinned at me over breakfast in the morning wearing last night's clothes. The peace came as if from nowhere, a light kiss on my neck when Pauline turned her back, a knowing look across the room when sex came on the television, a text that said

—*I miss you.*

or

—*You're my best friend.*

And that was the problem I guess. Or at least, that's what he said was the problem. That's why we couldn't be together, because we were friends and friends can't date but friends can fuck, and friends did fuck and the more they fucked the worse it became. Because I wanted him, and I wanted him to want me, and I wanted him to stop fucking other girls and I wanted to go upstairs without texting first and I wanted to lie on his bed and flick through his books and laugh about something that Pauline had said because we loved to tease her, and she loved when we did it. And I wanted to kiss him and hold his face between my hands and then go downstairs with the smell of him still on me and maybe his t-shirt too and I wanted to go into Pauline's room and sit on the edge of her bed and have her look at me with her big wide eyes and go

—Fuck off. No, you're joking, fuck off.

86

And I wanted Kyle to come down the stairs then too and knock on her door and say

—Are ye all decent?

And then Pauline would laugh and say

—I think you've already seen Char indecent.

And then he'd come in and he'd stand behind me and he'd put his hands on my shoulders and smile and Pauline would get out of bed and come to us and hug us both and we'd be one big fucked-up kind of family.

But instead, I'd creep downstairs in the morning and I'd slip into my room until one day I came down and Pauline was standing at the foot of the stairs and it was the morning after the night with Julia, because Kyle hadn't taken her upstairs and she'd gone home early and I hadn't fingered myself to the sound of their aggressive fucking but instead I'd let Kyle do it for me and Pauline looked angry so I said

—It's not what it . . .

But she didn't let me finish she just pointed at her room and I followed her in and she said

—I've known for ages. Everyone knows.

And I sort of smiled and she shook her head and said

—I dunno what you're smiling at. You're just going to get hurt again.

And I knew she was thinking about Dave and his body swinging from a scarf in his bathroom and I shrugged and I said

—It's complicated.

And it was.

YOU

I wait for you in the courtyard. I run my feet over the cobbled surface and pull my scarf tighter around my neck. It's November and it's getting cold, and all I can think about as I wait is bringing you back to my house later that evening, cuddling with you on my tiny couch as my storage heater crackles to life in the corner. I lean against one of the stone-cut cloisters, feel the chill of it through my coat, like the stone has soaked in the freeze of this early winter's day. A shadow falls across the courtyard from one of the balconies and that's when I see you. You walk towards me in a double-breasted navy-blue wool coat. You rub your hands together and blow on them.

—Dublin's so cold,

you say as you reach for me and pull me towards you by my waist.

I laugh and say

—Yeah, I heard there's a heatwave in Waterford.

You lift my body to yours, place your cold lips on me and suddenly we are leaning back against the cloister, but I can't feel the cold any more, all I can feel now is the wetness of your mouth on mine, all I can taste is peppermint over tobacco, a chewing gum attempt at disguising your last cigarette. You only smoked when you were drunk or nervous, that's what you'd told me. We eventually become unstuck, and I try to look you in the eye, but your gaze has already dropped to my feet. I guess in this moment, you were just as nervous as I.

We spend the day strolling around IMMA. We get lost in the latest artist installation, an ode to someone, or something, a time of war or peace or learning. I don't even know what we're looking at, can't comprehend. I'd normally be engrossed, have to be peeled away from each description on the tiny little placards beside the art, but today I am engrossed by you. Today, I can only see you, only try to understand you.

We get coffees from the little van that sits outside in the courtyard and you pay, pushing my hand back into my pocket. The cup warms my fingers and when you tell me I look beautiful I bring the cup to my face and blush behind it. I know my cheeks are red anyway, flushed from the changes in temperature, from inside the museum and out. We walk towards the gardens, down the grand steps and onto the gravel. There's a poetry pop-up in the Garden House that you've read about online. You seem excited to tell me, excited because you know it's something I'll like.

—It's called Poetry Speaks and it's like, all these different poets reading their stuff and like yeah, sounds cool.

I reach out and find your hand. My fingers slip into yours.

—There it is.

We approach the Garden House and see a large screen, we slowly start to hear voices and you're right, it is really cool. I love that you knew I'd like this. I love that we've only been dating two months and you already wanted to share my passions.

I love that you listened and I love being here, with you, on this bitter cold day, holding hands and watching poetry recitals on a big screen.

When it ends you squeeze my hand.

—Well, any good? I wouldn't have a clue about this kind of stuff to be honest.

I squeeze back and look down at our hands, our fingers intertwined.

—Yeah, really good, like really good.

And now I want to stay in this moment, standing here with you. I suddenly don't have the urge to take you home, take you from your clothes and take you to bed. Suddenly I just want to freeze time and be like this for ever.

—I could get used to this.

You smile as you roll onto your back.

—But, I'll never get used to those damn curtains.

I look at my window and I laugh.

—I know, I know, I need to get blinds or heavier curtains or something.

I place my palm on your chest, run my hand down to your belly.

—You should do it soon.

I yawn and nod my head.

—I mean, I'm not going to be able to sleep otherwise and if I can't sleep then how will I be able to get up and do interviews and all that? You know?

My hand movements stop, and I pull myself up onto my elbows.

—Sorry, what?

Your eyes are closed but there's a smile spreading across your face.

—Well, I'll need a good night's sleep before I go to my interviews.

I shake my head and lie onto your chest.

—Oh shut up.

You place a hand on my forehead.

—I'm serious Char.

I sit up again and this time your eyes are open.

—I want to be with you, like properly. I've finished the apprenticeship. I'm looking for a job anyway, why not Dublin?

—I mean, because you hate Dublin?

You look at me for a minute and the bed feels like it's spinning.

—Yeah, but I love you.

You close your eyes again quickly.

It's the first time either of us have said it. I want to scream. I want to cry. I want to get up and do an embarrassing victory dance in front of the mirror but I don't. I remain calm. I keep my cool. I bite down on my lip and I say

—I love you too.

When you get up to shower, I go to the mirror and wipe the blood from my lip.

I am loved. You love me.

You take me to Kerry for my birthday and I can't stop smiling for the entire drive down. We check into a fancy hotel and then you take me out for dinner. We share tacos and you lick the salt off the rim of a margarita like you're licking pussy.

That's what you say and it's so surprising and unlike you that I can't stop laughing.

You smile across the table at me, margarita held tentatively at your lips. I have to cross my legs together and squeeze my pelvic floor because even though it's funny, you are so stupidly sexy to me.

When we get back to the hotel, I run the bath. You call room service and order two pints of Guinness. I run my fingers through the white Molton Brown foam. The ensuite is warm, the running water fogging up the mirrors. I slip out of my dress, peel off my bra, and sit on the edge of the bath in a lace thong. I feel sexy. I feel beautiful. I feel alive. I'm tipsy and so are you but I still feel in control. I still feel like we have a handle on things, like the night won't escalate, run away with us, degenerate. And I'm right, it doesn't. It stays like this, a sort of romantic, domestic bliss. You answer the door and collect our pints and when you come into the bathroom, I'm lowering my body into the bath.

—I may have made it slightly too hot.

You put the pints on the side of the bath and test the water with your hand.

—Jesus Christ, are you trying to kill me?

I laugh, take a deep breath, and then lower myself down.

—It's okay, you get used to it.

You slip in opposite me, grimacing as you do, then you stretch out your legs and they surround me, and you pass me my drink.

—You're right actually, it's nice.

We clink glasses and then we both relax into the bath. You close your eyes and that's when I notice, you're smiling.

KYLE

The Malibu is probably curdling in my stomach at this point because I've drunk so much but the sun is out and Pauline has her Spotify party playlist on and the guys from next door have dragged their BBQ onto the balcony and this is going to be the perfect end to second year. Kyle has been gone for the past week, probably home visiting his parents and to be honest I'm glad of the break. Pauline, of course, has used this time to sit me down and give me 'the talk'.

—You are aware he is using you?

I nod.

—Okay, well good, because besides skipping most of your lectures and scraping by, I know that you are a smart girl.

I start to laugh but her face tells me that this isn't laughing season.

—I'm serious Charlotte. I watched you with . . .

She pauses and touches her face before she says his name.

— . . . Dave . . . and look . . .

She reaches over the kitchen table and touches my arm.

—That obviously was more . . . complicated than I realised but . . .

I'm waiting for her to get to her point and I've stuck a sort of pissed-off, go on say it but be careful, face on.

—I'm not gonna let you get hurt like that again.

She comes round the table and sits beside me.

—I don't mean like *that* obviously but, you know.

—You're comparing our housemate to my ex-boyfriend who hanged himself.

I even surprise myself with the coldness of it.

—That's not what I'm saying,

Pauline gushes.

—Then what are you saying?

—He uses you. You know this. You just admitted it. And I just can't face you going through another heartbreak, Charlotte.

—So, it's all about you?

I raise my hands and fake confusion. Pauline gets up and leaves the room. I know exactly what she means. I know that she's only looking out for me but I just don't want to accept it so I decide to play dumb, play the dead ex-boyfriend card and continue living my nightmare.

She seems to get over it by the weekend however and when Zach and Avery ask us to join them for the BBQ, she gets excited and goes to the off-licence so we can 'make proper cocktails'.

By 4 p.m. I'm bored waiting for her to perfect her pina coladas and take one of the multiple bottles of Malibu and go sit on the balcony chatting to Zach and Avery. Soon other people start arriving and we open the latch between the two balconies, and everyone starts to mingle.

By 6 p.m. I'm royally pissed.

I'm leaning back against the balcony railing listening to Zach having a debate on feminism and equality with some blond girl when I see him appear, Kyle. He comes in through our kitchen with a short, tired-looking girl in tow. She has nude lipstick on. I stand up straight, clutching the now empty bottle of Malibu by the neck. He walks slowly through the kitchen and out onto the balcony. A few people turn around and say hi but I just stare straight at him. I see Pauline get up from her seat on the balcony floor and approach him.

—This is Claire,

he says.

—We know who she fucking is.

Pauline is unsteady on her feet from too many badly made pina coladas and our friend Miriam jumps up laughing and says

—Sorry, she's a bit . . . let's go upstairs, yeah Pauline.

Miriam takes Pauline by the arm and leads her back into the kitchen but not before I catch her eye.

—I told you,

she mouths.

My hands are sweaty from the heat and the alcohol and the bottle starts to slip from my fingers.

—And tell me Kyle, who exactly is Claire?

I look at the girl standing sheepishly beside Kyle. I imagine her standing in our kitchen, Kyle covering her eyes, I imagine her walking from his bedroom in the late mornings, yawning, wearing his t-shirt.

—It's his ex-girlfriend.

I shout it more than say it and there's a sudden silence on the balcony.

I can hear a few mumbles behind me, maybe even a snigger.

—What? No, what?

Kyle is stuttering and turning to look at Claire. He goes to grab her hand but she pulls it away.

—I'm his girlfriend.

She says it firmly and I realise that this is the first time I've heard her speak. The first time I've really noticed her as an actual human.

I look at them both as the Malibu bottle finally slips from my fingers and crashes onto the floor.

—Jesus fucking Christ,

I say as I push past them and go into the kitchen.

I'm so drunk that I find it hard to make my way to my bedroom but when I do I see Miriam and Pauline arguing in the hallway.

Pauline turns to me.

—Now. Now do you fucking see?

—They've probably just gotten back together . . . I . . . it's not . . .

I can't finish my sentence because I don't know what the sentence is.

—I'm going back down there. I'm going back down to that absolute . . .

Miriam holds Pauline firmly but lovingly.

—You don't want to do this, not now, not after drinking, not in front of all our friends.

—Why? Shouldn't they all know what absolute scum he is?

Pauline's chest is heaving as she says it.

—I think they probably do.

All three of us turn around to see where the words have come from and see Claire standing at the end of the hall.

—How, how long have you two been . . . ?

She directs the question at me, brutal and clear.

I sigh and lean back against the wall.

—A while.

I slump onto the floor.

—And it hasn't just been me.

Claire scoffs then brings her hand to her mouth and starts to cry.

Pauline rushes forward and puts her arms around her.

—Don't cry, don't you dare cry for that scumbag.

Miriam stands back and watches the sorry scene.

A few minutes later Kyle appears in the hallway with Zach by his side.

—Get out, get the fuck out.

Pauline is shouting, Claire is still crying, and I'm hiding my face.

—I think you better . . .

Miriam opens the door and gestures out into the hallway.

—Come on guys, isn't there . . .

Zach tries to alleviate the tension but Pauline goes for him.

—Are you serious? Are you on his fucking side now?

Miriam grabs Kyle's arm and pulls him outside. Zach follows as Pauline screams after them.

—Yeah, and stay out you toxic pieces of masculine shit.

When everything went to hell, Kyle disappeared for days. It was nearly the end of term anyway but he still had a few exams to sit so I knew he would have to come back at some point. Nobody was speaking to him. Nobody wanted to. I felt his absence. He had planted himself deep inside me and his pain grew and unfolded with each passing day, I felt it in my gut. Then one day, passing the kitchen I saw him standing over the sink, his eyes fixated on something outside the window. There was never anything outside our window. I stepped into the kitchen and he didn't look up. I walked towards him and put my hands around his waist, leaned into him, rested my head on his back. The sweet, familiar smell of cardamom on his dressing gown. He touched my hands with his, damp and warm from the washing-up.

—Why are you being nice to me?

His voice cracked and I knew he was about to cry. I brought my fingers to his face, felt his cheek as a tear rolled down and I caught it. I didn't answer because there was no answer.

It wasn't long after this that Pauline came into the kitchen and ran towards me, palms cold as she pressed them to my face.

—Oh honey, oh honey.

They'd just pulled Kyle's body from the Liffey that afternoon and it still wasn't confirmed if it was an accident or a suicide.

—Oh honey. First Dave, now Kyle. I'm so sorry.

She closed her eyes and pulled my body into hers.

I decided now wasn't the time to tell her about Lar and Johnny too.

YOU

We were dating three months when I told you about my sister. My sister who died when I was twelve and she was sixteen. The bereavement was such a sudden blow to the family that we never fully recovered. I remember at twelve years old, thinking how much easier it would be if she had died in early childhood, how there was something that seemed more tragic about someone dying who was on the cusp of adulthood, about to begin their life. I remember thinking how it would have been better if I had died, a thought my mother, in the height of her grieving, had agreed with. Afterwards she apologised and said she didn't mean it and I told her that I accepted the apology, because I did, but I also knew that although my mother would never wish me dead, she would have happily traded me in to have Saoirse back.

My father said little before the death and after, nothing at all. The loss aged him and his body haunted the house now, a slow-moving silhouette who stayed mostly in the shadows.

You were shocked and sympathetic when I told you, all of the things I could have expected you to be. You were perfect, like you were about everything and suddenly I felt I could tell you anything, that you would understand it all.

Saoirse had been the pretty one, the clever one, the popular one – all of the attributes I did not possess, Saoirse exuded. But I was never jealous, instead I looked up to her, the way her arms flailed in excited gesticulation, the way her lips rounded into a pout when she was listening, the way boys came to our front door multiple nights a week to ask her out or bring her gifts. Saoirse's room was full of mixtapes made by love-struck teenage boys and together we lay on her bed, heads resting on our hands, ankles in the air, listening to the compilations.

I was ten when Saoirse met her first boyfriend, a tall, lanky boy with soft yellow curls. He was textbook good-looking but lacked a personality and when he came to our house he was quiet and stood coyly by the kitchen table waiting for Saoirse to appear. My mother would ask him questions, tell him she'd seen him at the hurling match the previous weekend and that he'd played a good game and he smiled demurely, looking at his feet as my father scratched his ear, observing from a distance.

When Saoirse finally appeared, she was always dressed conservatively, an unspoken deal between her and my mother that if she behaved a certain way then she could have a boyfriend.

I waited in the hallway and as my parents bid Saoirse and her boyfriend farewell I slipped a red lipstick into Saoirse's pocket on her way out the front door. My remuneration for this sneaky act was when Saoirse came home, pushed open my bedroom door and crawled into bed beside me. She rubbed my hair out against the pillow and I said

—Go on.

And she began her story.

—Okay so tonight we went to the Pitch and Putt and Chloe was there and you will never guess what she said.

Some nights her breath smelled sourly of alcohol or cigarettes but I chose to ignore this and lay in bed, Saoirse's legs wrapping around mine, cold from being outside and I listened to the stories of what it was like to be a woman.

Of course I didn't tell you all of this, I didn't see the point. I know you wanted to know more, I know you wanted to hear it all but I wasn't able. All I gave you were the cold hard facts. My parents, in their late forties, had buried their firstborn and none of us have ever really gotten over it.

Sometimes at night when I lie and think of you, your broad shoulders or the curve of your neck, I imagine Saoirse is lying next to me, I can feel her breath on my cheek and this time she says

—Go on.

And I twist onto my side and I'm about to tell her all about you, but when I turn, her body is not there and that's when I realise, neither are you.

ADAM

I see the taxi from my window. Adam calls.

—I'm outside, I think.

I see him close the door and look up at the hotel. He's wearing an Adidas tracksuit. It's kind of cute, I guess. Casual but cute.

—Yeah, you're here. I'll come down.

I check myself in the mirror. I may have overdone it, tight dress, heeled boots. I consider putting on a pair of dark tights but he calls again.

—*I'm coming, I'm coming.*

I step into the foyer and see him standing at the door, glancing around sceptically.

We hug awkwardly and I'm glad I've had three glasses of wine already.

—Let's just get to your room, yeah,

he says.

—Well you're fucking eager.

Pauline had told me that this was what I needed. Just some harmless Tinder fun.

—You just need to like, have some fun, you know?

She was right. The last few relationships had been intense.
I needed a break. I needed to mess around with some cute
Northerner and have a good time like a normal twenty-two-
year-old.

—You drunk?

Adam leans back against the mirror in the lift and grins
at me.

—I've had a glass or two of wine.

We reach the fourth floor and I lead the way to my room.

—So, you gonna tell me that this is your first time? That
you're not that type of girl and all that?

I'm struggling to open the heavy hotel door, but I manage
to turn around and smile.

—Oh no, I do this all the time. I usually charge though.

He grins back at me and we make our way into the room.
It smells of hairspray and fake tan and my make-up is spread
across the counter, clothes piled on the chair.

—Tidy.

—Fuck off.

I sit on the bed and pour myself another glass.

—You want some?

—I'll take a glass.

Adam produces a bottle of rosé from inside his jacket.

—But this is the shit I drink.

He reaches over and takes a glass from the bedside table.
He pours a large glass of rosé and lies back onto the bed, balancing the glass on his chest.

—So, you gonna tell me your deal or what?

I kick off my boots and pull my feet onto the bed.

—Tell you what?

—Your deal. You match with some guy on Tinder and you travel all the way to Belfast to see him and agree to meet him in some hotel room?

—Yeah.

Adam sits up and takes a drink.

—Yeah? That's all you're gonna give me?

—Well, what do you want me to say? My last four boy-friends all died or something?

Adam laughs.

—Yeah, something like that. I mean that would kind of explain it. You kill them or something?

I take another drink, then I reach across and touch Adam's cheek.

—Yeah, I fucked them to death.

When I pull off his top, Adam's body is smooth and slender and as I rub my fingers down his chest I feel his muscles move beneath. I feel every bone, every sinew. Feel his ribs as he breathes in and lies back onto the bed. His arms have small white lines just above the wrist, little scars, and I move my mouth over them, feel the uneven ridges against my lips. His fingers are long and stir as I move above him.

I feel large and heavy in comparison to his slight body. I feel clumsy until he holds my face in his hands and kisses my neck. I feel awkward and fat until he moves his hands down my body, cups my breasts.

We spend the night like this, wrapped in each other, in and out of sleep. We learn the shapes of each other and mould to fit them. In the morning I wake to sweat perco-lating between my lower back and his belly. Adam's hand is gripped beneath my right breast and his legs are intertwined in mine. I feel them jerk, testing him in his sleep. I move and so does he.

He wakes then and pulls me back into his body. He holds me tight and we become one. He's warm and sweaty and his hand clasps itself around my neck, my mouth. I make noise, muffled through his fingers and my teeth reach for his skin; I bite down but he doesn't react. Doesn't retract. His other hand now on my lower back, pushing me forward.

When we finish, he showers and I lie with the sheets off poking at an ingrown hair on my upper thigh.

—My phone in there?

I pass it to him and he plays music loudly in the bathroom and when he comes back I'm wearing his t-shirt, standing by the window. We don't hug or kiss. Our intimacy has ended. Adam lights two cigarettes, one for me and one for him. Now we laugh and talk and when we lean out the window, me perched on the windowsill, Adam singing to me, passers-by look up, hear the music and they must think we've been out all night, an after-party.

We don't know each other. Not properly. But we are connected by this need. This desire.

He throws the cigarette out the window and sits back on the bed. I go to him and I stand in front of him and his mouth traces my outline. He's smiling and I can feel it, on my hip, on my thigh. He pulls my clothes from me and I stand naked, sun breaking through the curtains, morning coming in fast. His hands are rough as they slide down my legs and as I climb onto the bed, onto him, he lies back, still smiling. The sheets are still wet from last night but we don't care and we make love as morning songbirds rise outside the hotel window. We make love, music. And all the time, I don't know if I'll ever see him again. All the time, I wonder if I'll ever see him again.

YOU

I thought that we were perfect, but then, perfection doesn't exist and sometimes when we drank, it was always when we drank, my past would come to haunt me, hover over me like an apparition and I would have to drink to unsee it. The dead bodies, the matted hair, the deep wounds. And on those nights, I was a mess. I could feel the intoxication come for me like a wave and I swam into it, drowned in it.

I remember one night, about a year into our relationship, the weekend after you'd gone out with the boys and bumped into your ex. She'd stood by the bar alone, you'd said, and fingered a plastic straw in an empty glass. She'd spoken to you, but she'd been drunk and you hadn't understood her. You just wanted me to know that she was there, that she had come all the way from Waterford to Dublin with some friends and happened to be in the same club as you that night. You just thought it was best not to keep these things from me. And I'd felt a familiar sinking in my stomach but I'd ignored it and was happy when Cian said he was coming to Dublin for the weekend and you'd agreed to come out with us.

We got ready in our apartment and I'd sat cross-legged on the sofa, flicking through Grindr trying to set him up and you'd mixed our drinks and Cian had tasted his, grimaced and exclaimed

—Are you trying to kill us or what?

And I'd laughed but then I'd felt the past and it was nudging me now, asking me to turn around, to look back, to sink into memories, cajoling me. So, I downed the drinks and I felt the inebriation and it dulled the sirens of memory.

I don't remember getting to the club or being separated from you, but I do remember coming to in the middle of the upstairs lounge. And I remember watching as lights danced across bare shoulders and I swayed out of time to the music, to a tune that was beating in my own head.

And the club moved with me, steadily heaving up and down. And I felt like we were in a pinball machine and the bodies were little silver balls, the DJ playing music that scattered the balls all over the floor. And I was one of them being spun back and forth in this little box. I hit off the other balls and sent them flying.

There was a glass in my hand but I didn't know what I was drinking. All drinks tasted the same now, the sweet and sugary cola flavour soured by something else, something stronger. Something that made me walk funny as I approached the toilets. There was a queue and some girl turned around and looked at me. She had all this glittery highlight smeared across her forehead and it made her look sweaty. She said something through rouge-stained lips.

I smiled, my biggest, fakest smile.

—That's the men's honey.

I notice then that I am in fact queuing for the men's bathroom and this sweaty-foreheaded girl is pulling me into her queue. I know I should say thanks but I can't be bothered, besides, the words won't come out.

—Are you okay honey?

I'm glad I haven't thanked her now. I hate the name honey. I hate her.

I end up not using the toilet, instead, I stare into the mirror. I know that my reflection stares back at me but I can't really see it. The glass is blurry and my body looks distorted. I rub my fingers over my lips and feel the waxy residue of lipstick. I think that's better, think I've fixed it. I make my way back out of the toilets, pushing people out of my way.

—Drunk slut,

somebody shouts after me and I smile, I don't know why, but I find that funny.

You are here somewhere but I'm not with you. I'm on the stairs, the ones you told me that you and Paddy used to stand below to look up and see under girls' skirts. I hold the rail and look down to see if anyone below is looking up at me, to see under my skirt. I look down to see if you're there, if you're looking up but you aren't.

People move past me, fast and hard, their bodies aggressive and heavy. But I feel light like I could float down the stairs, like my body could lift itself high into the air and land somewhere below. Near you, perhaps.

I let go of the railing and I make my way down the steps. I drop my feet one after the other in exaggerated leaps and swing my arms. I feel sort of wonderful. Some guy in a black jacket, a big, burly fellow comes towards me.

—Careful love.

He grips my elbow like men are inclined to do when you get in and out of fancy cars and I grin at him.

—Thank you, kind sir.

He has something in his ear and he presses it. He's speaking now but not looking at me and I make my way through the machine, past all the little balls and diversions.

Then I hear my name. I spin around and there you are.

Your face is tanned and glowing but your lips are cracked and the patch above your upper lip looks sore and dry. I want to kiss you to soothe it but you're holding your phone in my face. A message lights up the screen. It's a message from your ex. I take the phone in my hand. The letters dance off your screen but I manage to read them.

—*Don't feel too bad about the other night, Charlotte is getting with some bald guy in Copper Face Jacks.*

I hand you back the phone and say

—Well I'm clearly not.

I place the palms of my hands out as some sort of indication of innocence. We decide she must be in the club and has seen me with Cian. I follow you upstairs. Maybe we're going to find Cian, I don't know.

When we do find him I rub my hand along his bald head and laugh. You're speaking to him intently and I can't remember why. I sit on a high stool near the bar and wait for you. You're so tanned in the half-light and your skin stands out against your crisp white t-shirt. You turn and look at me. You're smiling. You throw your arm around Cian, telling him all about what has just happened. Your fingers sit on his shoulder and they are rough and dark. You're laughing now and so is Cian, you have some private joke. I go to take a sip from my drink but my hands are empty. I try to move off my seat to go to the bar but you are holding me now, your firm hands digging into my sides. You tell me you think I've had enough, you call me honey.

Honey.

I twist my body in your grip and look at you. I look at your dry lips and green, speckled eyes.

—What did she mean?

You look at me confused.

—What did she mean? *Don't feel too bad about the other night.* What did you do?

Your ex hated me, as exes are wont to do, and I can't say I was her biggest fan either. It didn't help that you'd gone to school with her back in Waterford. It didn't help that she was best friends with all of your best friends. It didn't help that every weekend when you went home, she was there.

—What did she mean 'don't feel too bad'?

I sit up in bed, nursing my hangover from the night before, tracing my steps and making a mental note of everything that had happened. Of course I don't remember much and your ex texting was the only thing that seemed to stick.

—Jesus, not this again.

You roll over and turn your back to me.

—She thought you were getting with Cian. Let it go.

But I don't want to let it go, I can't let it go.

—I'm not talking about that, I'm talking about when she said, don't feel too bad, I'm talking about that part.

I touch your shoulder and my voice is low, friendly. I genuinely just want to know. You feel my fingers and jolt upright.

—For fuck's sake Charlotte. I can't do this. I can't deal with the constant jealousy and interrogations.

—But I . . .

I scramble for words, reasoning, as you get out of bed and pull on a t-shirt.

—I didn't mean . . .

You turn and look at me.

—I think I should go. I'm heading back to Waterford. I don't want to be with you right now.

—But you've got an interview tomorrow, you can't just go?

—I dunno Charlotte, honestly. But look, maybe, if you could just drop this nonsense with my ex then . . .

—I will, I'm sorry, I just . . .

You stand up.

—Okay, okay, I'll stay. But I'm going out for a run.

And you walk out of the bedroom, grabbing the keys from the bedside table, and I sink back into the pillow and I can feel my heart racing in my chest.

SAOIRSE

When Loretta Byrne came to me and said she didn't want to be my best friend any more, I cried. It was my first rejection and I took it hard, right there beside the 4th class Art Cart. A bottle of acrylic paint between my fingers, I squeezed so hard I felt the tube collapse in on itself and skyline blue dripped down my pinafore. Loretta dropped her wet brushes into the basin beside me and walked away, her ponytail swinging behind her as if it too was glad to be rid of me. It would probably have been okay if it wasn't for the fact that Loretta Byrne was the cool girl in our class and if she decided not to be your friend then it would transpire that you suddenly had no friends at all. Except maybe Weird Lucy, but that was social suicide, a fate nobody would even consider. Weird Lucy is now a happily married biology professor, so I guess we had her all wrong.

I wiped my hands on my legs above my knee socks as the paint clung to my shins, an animated-looking bruise. Mrs Forrester tut-tutted and pointed at the door, lowering her glasses in stereotypical teacher style. I walked out of the classroom and into the Junior bathrooms. I rolled a piece of toilet paper in my hand and held it under the hot tap, feeling the paper turn to a wet tissue. I scrubbed my knees, rolls of pilling paper barely removing the paint. It was mid-scrubbing that the tears came. The feeling of rejection a large ball in my throat now freed as I bawled into the sink.

—What the hell are you at?

I look up and see Saoirse standing in the doorway.

I bring my hands to my face to hide the tears but instead spread soggy toilet paper and acrylic paint onto my face.

—Jesus Christ almighty. Come here.

I drop the tissue into the sink and walk towards my sister. She spits on her hand and, holding my head forcefully, rubs my cheeks.

—What's going on?

—It's paint.

—Well, I can see that Char.

I look at the floor.

—Jesus Charlotte, you're not crying over spilling a bit of paint, are you? You seriously need to toughen up. You can't be going around crying over every little thing when I'm in the Vocational next year.

The tears resume and Saoirse pulls me into her arms.

—You're getting paint on your uniform.

I say it through muffled tears.

—I don't care about that. Now tell me, what happened you big eejit?

I somehow manage to spit out the word 'Loretta'.

—That little four-eyed fuck.

Saoirse rubs my back.

—Don't be crying over her.

When lunch came around Loretta's lunchbox was missing and she only found it at the end of the day, egg mayonnaise spoiling under the sun on the basketball court.

Saoirse was waiting for me at the gate.

—You want to go get ice cream, or will you cry over that too, you big baby?

ADAM

His friend is driving crazy fast and I can't tell if he's been drinking or not. I try not to think about it. I hold a bottle of Buckfast between my thighs in the back seat, the lid's gone, I don't know where and I squeeze tight to keep it from spilling. Adam keeps turning around and smiling at me. I don't know where we're going and I'm sure this can't be safe but his eyes are this stupid blue and when he smiles I get this feeling in my knees like I might collapse so I just cradle the bottle and smile back.

Lorraine sits beside me clutching her handbag to her chest and keeps giving me that stare. If I'd known she'd be such a buzzkill I wouldn't have invited her. Still, it felt better to have someone who knew Belfast in the car with me, it felt safer somehow. Lorraine had moved to Belfast to study at Queen's and I'd only come to visit once or twice. Our friendship had certainly faded since we left Coolfarnamanagh. But that was to be expected, I'm sure. We were just different people now, I wasn't using her, I pushed those thoughts firmly to the back of my mind.

The music is loud, electronic and it beats in my ears, in my head, aggressively infiltrating my mind. I raise my hand to my face, brushing loose strands of hair out of my eyes. I can still smell Adam on my skin.

Last night, after we'd had sex, we drank rosé and watched MTV while he lay across my lap and told me about his ex and his first time and all the girls in between. I told him about Kyle and he'd looked interested and impressed. We'd been messaging for weeks and I'd been building myself up to meeting him. I didn't think I'd go through with it. Didn't think I'd come up North to see him but in the end Pauline convinced me I should, convinced me I deserved it after all that drama with Kyle.

But now suddenly it's all real and I sit in his friend Jamie's car and he has this strong Northern accent and I can't understand him but I laugh when Adam laughs and that seems to work.

We fly along Cupar Way and Jamie lets the window down and leans out as he drives, one hand on the steering wheel.

—Oi sweetie.

A girl on the pavement turns to look at us as Jamie slows the car down.

—Geeeeeaaaaat your tits out for the laaaads.

The girl shouts obscenities back at us and Adam pulls Jamie's arm and tells him to cop on. I have this sinking feeling. I lift the Buckfast to my mouth and try to swallow as we glide over speed bumps and I end up with purple stains all down my top and sticky residue on my chin. I wipe my face with the back of my hand.

Jamie sits back into the driver seat properly now and I see his left hand reaching towards the glovebox.

—Nah man, no.

Adam pushes his hand away, but he just reaches for it again and the car swerves dangerously into the other lane.

—Alright, Jesus.

I see Adam open the glovebox and pull out a tiny bag of white powder.

—He's fucking coked?

I say it out loud by accident and they both turn around.

I can feel Lorraine stir beside me.

The car swerves again and Jamie turns back around to keep us on the road.

—Ach he's grand. Want some?

Adam shakes the bag in front of my eyes.

—Never mind her like, gimme.

Jamie swipes the bag from Adam's hand. He uses his elbows to steer and fumbles with the coke between his fingers.

—Jesus Christ.

Adam looks at me and rolls his eyes, then takes the bag from Jamie's shaking hand and sticks his little finger in, collecting the powder under his nail and then shoving it aggressively up his left nostril.

He offers me some again and I decline.

The car speeds through a residential area and I watch as the rows of small, semi-detached houses become one big blur of brick and mortar. I still don't know where we're going but it feels far.

We eventually pull into a housing estate and park outside someone's house. Perhaps it's Jamie's. I don't bother to ask, it seems irrelevant. We climb out of the car.

We end up sitting in a living room with six other guys and I learn that this is another one of Adam mates' houses. I'm wedged between Adam and some guy who keeps rubbing his knee against mine. Jamie sits on the armchair opposite us with Lorraine. She pulls her cardigan up around her face like she might catch something from breathing in the same air as these men.

—So how is the little slut?

Jamie directs the conversation at me.

—This little whore, yeah . . .

He looks around to make sure everyone is listening.

—She's been putting out for Adam *and* for me.

There's a ripple of laughter.

—Ain't that right sweetie?

—Yeah, and your mum as well but then, she puts out for everyone.

I feel Adam move beside me. Is he laughing? I can't tell. Why isn't he standing up for me? Why isn't he telling these people that I have never even met Jamie until this night.

—Low-blow Charlotte but then you'd know all about blowing low.

There's cheering in the room now and I don't want to be here. The guy beside me isn't laughing and he passes me a joint.

I don't want it but I feel so uncomfortable that I take it.

Jamie is looking at Adam now but Adam looks past him to Lorraine.

—So, what are you studying?

—Eh, political science,

Lorraine replies gingerly and I wonder why she's gone shy all of a sudden, is she really that intimidated by a handful of guys and a gram of coke? She was never this timid.

She relaxes in her seat slightly and lowers her cardigan. Adam leans forward in his seat.

—So you're like, smart?

She nods and I can see Adam smiling.

—Wow, that's impressive.

I feel weird then as I inhale the joint. I feel like something is off. I pass the joint back to Adam's quiet friend and he mutters something unintelligible. I realise that he's very fucking high and I hope that's not me in a few minutes.

—You are cute though, in fairness.

Jamie is looking at me as he says it and leans forward pulling the little bag of coke from his pocket. He tips the white powder from the bag onto the glass table in front of us. Then, pulling a card from his wallet, he starts dragging it into little mounds and then lines. He points the card at me from his hunched position.

—You want?

I shake my head as Adam's other friend passes me the weed again.

I smoke some more before I realise that Adam is no longer sitting beside me. He's sitting on the floor by Lorraine's feet.

—Your loss, this is some good shit.

Jamie rolls a five-pound note and snorts a line. He throws his head back dramatically and screeches.

—Yabadabadoo!

I can feel everyone in the room getting annoyed at him. Adam kicks him gently, stretching his foot out from his new position on the floor.

Jamie doesn't seem to mind the animosity that hangs in the air. Adam glares at him. But Jamie isn't looking at Adam, he's looking at me and his eyes wash over me, bathing my body with his warm, persistent gaze. He grins, a wide, toothy thing, and sticks out his tongue, pinching it between his teeth. I almost grin too but then I look at Adam, look at how his body has manoeuvred closer to Lorraine, look at Lorraine rub her knuckles against her cheek, which I know is her body's signature flirting move.

I'm getting annoyed now. Annoyed at Adam for sitting so close to her, annoyed at Lorraine for having the audacity to nervous-giggle around him and annoyed at myself for ever coming on this trip in the first place.

Adam throws his head back in animated laughter, Lorraine chews a nail.

A swirl of smoke dances in front of my eyes from the joint.

—Well, it's hardly that fucking funny.

Everyone turns to look at me. Adam is lying back and Lorraine is now seated on the floor beside him, head resting on his shoulder. I realise that some time has elapsed since the joke, and the weed fog starts to descend.

—What?

It's Jamie who speaks next and I can see him dragging more cocaine into lines on the table. His head bobbles on his shoulders and looks like it doesn't quite fit his body.

—The joke . . .

I pass the joint back to the guy beside me, whose name I still don't know, and try to sit up. The task appears too much for my lethargic body and I just slump back against the cushions.

—You're a joke.

Jamie smiles as he says it and I smile back, watching his head, searching for the invisible spring.

—Well, you're a fucking . . . yoke.

It takes some effort to say the words and I close my eyes for respite. Next, I feel a clammy hand on my forehead and Jamie says

—Yup, as I expected, high temperature and you know, mania.

My eyes open and Jamie is seated back in his chair, he's playing some loud house track on his iPhone and the phone balances between his shoulder and his ear. The tinny vibration fills the room.

—Mania?

Jamie looks at me and laughs.

—Welcome back then.

I pull my body forward and look around. My friend with the joint is no longer beside me. Adam and Lorraine are no longer seated on the floor. The room feels dense, heavy.

—Where's Adam?

Jamie drops his phone onto his lap and leans forward.

—Ah! Well now, how can I put it?

My eyes search the room again but it is most definitely just me and this cokehead.

—Just where is he? And where's Lorraine and everyone?

—How about just a baby line? Basically you won't be high at all.

Jamie gestures to the cocaine that still litters the table and picks up his Co-op card.

—I don't want any fucking cocaine.

I rise to my feet now, head dizzy and legs unsure.

—Well excuse me for breathing! And look at you now, missus sleepyhead no more. You realise you've been passed out for like forty-five minutes like?

I shake my head and ease myself back into the seat.

—I don't feel good.

Jamie nods, as if in agreement.

—The white stuff, greatest cure going.

—I highly doubt that.

There's a moment of silence and Jamie leans forward. He places a rolled five-pound note to his nose and the line of powder disappears into the vacuum. I can almost hear it move through his nose, past the mucous membranes and hair. He throws the note down, throws his head back and sniffs hard. Then he licks his forefinger, places it into his nostril and then back into his mouth.

He sees me staring.

—Waste not, want not, aye?

I roll my eyes in disinterest but curl my lip in disgust.

—They left together, didn't they?

Jamie wipes his hand on his jeans and nods his head.

—Aye. But here, that Adam is a pussy boy, don't be worrying about him.

I lie back and feel the nausea ensue. Buckfast and weed do not a good combo make.

—One bump?

I look up and see Jamie standing over me with a small pile of cocaine on his finger.

—You can just rub into your gums like. No need to snort it.

He sits on the seat beside me and I turn to him.

—Ugh fine. But I'll pick it up myself thanks. If I die, I want it to be from the cocaine, not some faecal matter that got stuck on your finger when you were scratching your arse earlier.

He smiles as I pull the table closer.

—You dirty bastard,

I add for good measure.

I lick my finger and stick it into one of the mounds.
—Takes one to know one,
Jamie says, rubbing his hands together.
Is there a word for pre-emptive regret?

The night bled into morning and straight into the following night. The palpitations in my chest drove me onward, through the hours. We pulled curtains on the rising sun and waited for the security blanket of night. The cocaine was sharp and fizzing in my veins. It flowed through me, a persistent buzz. My jaw ached and my tongue was dry, my lips chewed and bleeding.

Jamie's spirit came to life and he was large, larger than before, an entity that grew and was now towering above us. And we drank large glasses of water and we talked with an ardent fervour, words that seemed to rhyme, words that were lyrical and seductive to the ear.

And his hands were on me or around me and they were sweaty and clammy all at once and we were hot and we were cold, constantly dressing and undressing. And the cocaine made me comfortable to strip to my bra and Jamie's eyes, so focused on my mouth and my gesticulating, never ventured to my chest.

We did a lot of cocaine, Jamie doing the most and I was mildly anxious that we had gone too far. And the anxious thoughts materialised as bodily tics, flexing my fingers, cracking my knuckles and licking my sore lips. But the deep feeling of loss and abandonment from the night before was heightened now and it outshone my worry and I looked at myself in the bathroom mirror and Jamie licked his palms and smoothed my hair and we were beautiful.

The distorted reflection showed our two bodies as apparitions, a sight for only God to admire and we believed this. Our eyes were wide, pupils black and deep and ominous. But our smiles were wider, bigger, greater and our teeth, though sore and heavy in our mouths, were white and straight and gleaming.

We looked at ourselves and then each other and Jamie held the powder on his finger and I inhaled, felt the substance tear through my nose, tight and compact it moved through the nasal passage and then released itself into whatever cavity would have it, it was reborn then and it was wild and free. And the cheap constitutions it was cut with evaporated and the drug flourished inside me and I was illuminated from within.

And Jamie kept saying my name and it sounded rich and opulent on his tongue and I felt a sense of wonderment at my own beauty.

We had heard people come home at 4 a.m. but we were in the bathroom, grooming ourselves and each other and I had almost forgotten about Adam and Lorraine as I sat cross-legged on the tiled floor, willing the coldness to enter my bones. It wasn't until 9 a.m. that we encountered the other bodies that roamed the house. They all seemed tired and hungover, a heavy weight pressing against the backs of their eyes, sore muscles and joints and we smiled at them and they shook their heads and drank coffee and water and ignored us. In the afternoon we played music loudly on the television and Adam's friend, the one who owned the house, leaned over the table and snorted a line of coke and soon he was standing on the table and had joined us in song. Then the others appeared, like the resurrected Lazarus and we were all high and happy and ready.

It wasn't until late evening that Adam arrived with Lorraine in tow and by this point I had gone past any sense of sobriety. I had lapsed into moments of coming down all throughout the previous night and morning but now I was drinking Jägermeister and I had adjusted to the cocaine levels in my body and all I felt was happiness.

I looked at the pair as they stood in the doorway and I felt Jamie's hand on my back and I recognised the weight of it and I smiled at Lorraine and I called her forward.

—It's not what you think.

I put my arm around her and I could feel the warmth of her body seep into my own. I brought my face to her shoulder and I breathed her in.

—It's fine.

She pulled away from my grasp and looked at me. She seemed worried and so I held her hand and brought her to the bathroom.

Once there, I turned the lock in the door and we both sat on the tiles now covered in ashes and cigarette butts from my previous night's antics.

—He's an asshole,

she said and brought her hand to her face to cover the tears that were now erupting.

—I know. Trust me I know.

I placed a hand on her thigh and I could feel my body shaking.

—If anyone knows, I know.

I was shouting now but I couldn't help it. My legs were restless and I jumped to my feet. I started a light jog on the spot and I rubbed my hands down my thighs.

—What are you doing?

Lorraine looked up at me from her place on the floor and her eyes seemed deeper now and I noticed for the first time that they were an unearthly blue.

—Your eyes. Jesus, your eyes.

I got down on my hunkers and bobbed silently in front of her.

—Charlotte, you need to sober up. I need to tell you what happened.

I rocked back onto my buttocks then and stretched out below the sink. I looked up at the contortions of pipes and drains and I smiled.

—It doesn't matter, I forgive you.

Lorraine slapped my legs, causing me to sit up sharply. The room spun.

—Forgive me?

She looked at me vehemently.

—Forgive me? You want to forgive me?

I didn't reply and I watched as she folded her head into her body, sobbing.

—If anything, it should be me forgiving you,

she muttered under her breath.

I reached forward and put my fingers underneath her chin. I lifted her head. The intense buzzing in my head lessened and I used my other hand to ground myself and stop my body shaking.

—What happened Lorraine?

I looked at her face as I asked and I suddenly knew that whatever the answer, I would feel it more definitely than I had ever felt anything before.

YOU

My desire for you was a demon that lived inside me. I wondered if you knew it, knew her, this beast that lived within me. This devil that possessed me. I brought her from my sleep into my waking world and walked beside her now. She held my hand.

When the first drops of blood dampened my inner thigh, when all the feeling went from my head to my toes and I almost collapsed onto my desk, she was there, hovering in the background, ready to grab me and take me.

I'd run my hand between my legs, feel the parts of me that I'd never thought to feel before. And then I imagined all sorts of things. Things I'd never seen or experienced but things I imagined happened behind closed doors and in the back of cars with foggy windows.

I looked at teachers, male, female and I imagined their naked flesh, bursting and brimming and spilling out of their clothes. And it was the women first, whose ample chests sat at eye level as they bent over explaining a question, it was their breasts that I imagined first, touching and feeling and putting my face against them.

Because I understood their body, and so, as I rubbed the space between my legs, the space that I came to know and love and hate all at the same time, I gripped one breast with my left hand and I squeezed and I wished it were bigger.

I thought of it like a flame, this burning, rising yearning and I imagined that having sex would extinguish it. I imagined losing my virginity would calm me, stifle the thoughts of wet lips and roaming tongues, but it only made it worse.

The desire grew to addiction and I sought it with a ferocity that consumed me. I took it with me into every relationship and that was fine, that was helpful, that was the fuel that kept us going. But it did not stand alone and when everything else crumbled away, this fire, this light, remained flickering against the darkness.

When I first discovered how to please myself, I was embarrassed, I was ashamed. I was filled with that great Catholic guilt and although I didn't believe that I would go blind, I did feel dirty. So I had to find someone, I had to share this need and men came and men provided and soon the act was collaborative, connected, championed. And they loved it, they loved how I pursued them in this way, how I fulfilled this considered masculine need.

And you loved it and it was okay when I was with you. It was safe. It was controlled.

But now that you are gone, I fear the demon.

ADAM

Lorraine cried all the way through her story and I held her in my arms on the bathroom floor. I could hear the others leaving for the club so I rubbed her cheeks and said
—We don't have to go.
She looked at me, exhausted.
—I want to.
—But he's going to be there Lorraine. Are you sure?
She looked at me and nodded and I was so high I agreed.

The club was dark, the air dense, the music heavy. Reverberations of the beat that you could feel in your stomach. High pitches of laughter, sweaty palms, wide eyes. Cold, waxy walls with condensation. Dark, sticky floors, misty air, the ebb and flow of bodies.

I held Lorraine's hand as we moved through the crowd. I felt her vulnerability seep through her fingers and onto my skin. I felt it move along my arm as we pushed past bodies, as we pinched our limbs tight to fit through crowded spaces. I felt her vulnerability like a thick emollient on my skin. It was soothing, almost protective, like everything she had experienced, everything she felt had somehow eased my pain and suffering. I felt this and I felt bad. And the guilty feeling, this feeling of having escaped, turned to anger and my grip tightened on Lorraine and she returned the squeeze and together we turned vulnerability into revolt.

We'd arrived with Jamie, two hours after Adam had left with the others. We'd told them we'd meet them here, in the club and when we arrived Jamie went in search of his friends. Lorraine and I went to the bathroom and I'd held her by her shoulders, tempted to shake her wildly, but I'd resisted. I'd wiped her brow free of sweat. I'd held her head back and dropped eye drops that Jamie had given me to help my own cocaine situation into her eyes.

She'd bent her knees slightly and tilted her head back. She'd closed her lips tightly and opened her eyes. She'd looked up at me and her pupils were large, adjusting to the darkness of the club. The deep blue of her irises seemed to swim as I leaned over her face. I looked into their depths, a hazy reflection of myself looking back at me. The drops fell slowly from the container, emulsifying when they hit the aqueous membrane. Lorraine's eyelids reacted quickly then and she blinked rapidly. She stood up straight and wiped the escaping liquid off her cheeks and she hugged me and I stood still, let the embrace linger.

Now we were on a mission. Now we were going to find Adam, now we were going to confront him. We hadn't really discussed what we were going to say or do, we just knew that we would do it together. There had been a part of me that had wanted to go to the police but Lorraine had stayed firm on that point, she was not reporting it, she couldn't. Her memory of the previous night was fuzzy, she'd been drunk and there had been a lot of drugs passed around. She'd fallen asleep in his bed and she couldn't be entirely sure what had happened but when she woke, she was sore and Adam slept next to her and they were both naked. She knew that she wasn't sober enough to consent but she also wasn't sober enough to relay the information to the authorities. So I'd agreed that we would confront him together.

Now, walking through the club, looking for his face amid a sea of twenty-something-year-olds I started to worry. What were we going to do?

I looked back and saw Lorraine following me sheepishly, hand swinging as she clutched my fingers. She looked so childish, so innocent now, that the anger reappeared and I quickened my pace, scanning the room for the spineless prick.

We couldn't find him on the dancefloor so we went back to the bar where Jamie was once again at large ordering shots for everyone in sight.

—Charlotte, hen, c'mere.

He stretched out his arms and pulled me towards him.

—Sambuca? Tequila? What are you having?

His jaw was swinging, his eyes beaming and I knew he had now taken something else.

—I'm okay.

—Ye are in yer bollocks. Here, what's your name, what do you want?

He directed the next question at Lorraine, who moved forward and leaned on the bar.

—Or do you only take drinks off yer fella, Adam?

I swung my leg at Jamie and hit him in the shin.

—Shut the fuck up.

He looked at me and appeared bemused.

—Alright, calm down. Jesus, can yer wee friend not take a joke?

I looked at Lorraine to see her reaction but she didn't even appear to have noticed.

—Three tequilas, good lad.

Jamie was brandishing a twenty-pound note in the air. He turned to me grinning.

—Alright, tequila is it. Cheer up there buttercup.

I lifted the fat shot glass to my lips and poured the tequila into my mouth. The sharp sting of alcohol on my throat and the subsequent aftertaste made me shake my head and Jamie laughed. He placed his arm around me then and pulled me into an embrace.

—You know hen, you're alright.

Then he brought a tightly furled fist in front of my face. He slowly opened it and I saw three white pills sitting on his palm.

—Reckon you could handle?

I pushed his hand away and looked around, the paranoia now kicking in.

—For fuck sake Jamie.

He laughed and using his fingers he popped the three pills into the waistband of my trousers. He slapped my arse hard then and winked at me before walking away.

—Now one is for your wee friend there and I'll be back for one later. Don't take the three of them yerself,

he shouted as he walked away.

—What would happen if I took the three of them?

He put his hands out to declare ignorance.

—I dunno, but I'd say you'd fairly die.

I rubbed the waistband and felt the three pills sitting against my underwear. I looked at Lorraine, now slumped against the bar, her head in her arms.

—Come on,

I said, lifting her body.

—Where are we going?

If you read the *Belfast Telegraph* the following day, you'd have read how a young man had died of an ecstasy overdose in the very club we'd been in. His name was Adam. But of course, I didn't see that article. Nobody I know did.

YOU

The summer we met was beautiful.

You always drove with the windows down.

Your hands were soft and as you reached out for my leg I reclined in the seat and we drove out of Dublin.

The fields rolled past, the signs, JJ Kavanagh buses. The sun now right in our eyes, we could barely see the road. You'd reach over and unclip my visor. Your hands were tanned, fingers familiar and every vein from wrist to elbow I knew and venerated.

Your body was holy.

You wore shorts that you rolled up and white trainers, kept perfectly clean. You wore a grey t-shirt, and you always asked me to roll the sleeves so they sat just at your shoulder.

I loved when we drove to Waterford to visit your family. It made it all feel so solid, secure.

We walked hand in hand and I was terribly smug. I had you, a vision of beauty to my untrained eye.

I had been through some of the worst years of my life but now I had you, everything was going to be alright.

We sat on grass, ate grapes, threw bread to the notoriously flighty swans. We lay in bed, windows open, pollen sneaking in and settling beneath my nose, and you laughed as I sneezed, and you held me through the night. We were naked, we were clothed, we were lost and found.

We were floating through that summer.

Your family accepted me and I them and soon we were one. You'd wash my hair in their shower and I'd grip your waist, feel the suds run down my back, slide off my bum. Your hands were velvet as they ran through my hair and my whole body was for you. I was proud of every inch, every part of me, because you said it was yours. And it was. So we morphed into one, a duo. I held the tissue to your nose when it bled, you brushed your teeth with my toothbrush. There were no boundaries.

At night we came alive, and our bodies never failed to excite one another. We were filled with love, adrenaline. You were strong and could hold me, lift me, raise me and I was weakened by you. I faltered at your feet. I adored you.

Those summer days turned into months, years and fast-forward to Dublin, both of us, living together, working together, being . . . together.

Is that when it all went wrong? Is that when you fell out of love with me? Was it over even before you met her? Was it over before you decided to move home?

I stood in the doorway, I looked at you.

—Don't go.

But you did and we both knew, we must have known, that this was the end. Even as you held my hand over drinks at Sophie's rooftop bar. Even as a tear fell from your green eye, even as you swore never to stop loving me. We knew, didn't we? We knew this was the end. You were moving back to Waterford, Dublin had failed you and I felt I had failed you too.

But I never imagined her. I never imagined you'd have someone else, and I cried and I screamed and I wanted to pull every strand of her hair from her head when I saw it.

I was on yard duty when you changed your WhatsApp photo and she was there all smiles and grins and every kid in the basketball court could have been struck down by an armed maniac and I wouldn't have even noticed, I probably wouldn't have even cared.

So I kept thinking about that summer. The summer we met and the endless conversations, and the trips to the museum and your hands all over me. Your eyes intense and your lips devouring.

I imagined all those nights in my single bed, no sleep just you and me exploring each other, endless possibilities. And you loved me. You said it, so often, so loud. You loved me and you held me and you loved me all night long and again in the morning. And how, how could she replace that?

I kept thinking of that day I got the train to Waterford to see you. And you looked at me and said,

—What are you doing here?

But I stayed and you drove us back to your house.

And the sun dropped in the sky and a yellow hue hung over Waterford. It was warm that summer too, four years after our first, and I could feel the heat at the back of my knees as I sat shaking in the seat beside you.

You drove with the windows down, music loud, blaring, setting me on edge.

Your hands were soft as you reached for my leg. You pulled into a lane and pulled me into the driver's seat and we made love and after you looked at me disgusted and said

—That meant nothing.

And then the sun was set, and we drove in darkness, out of the city.

SAOIRSE

Saoirse swings my bedroom door open and walks to the IKEA mirror hanging by the window.

—It's so unfair that your room gets all the good light. We should swap.

I'm stretched out on my bed applying stickers to my nails in an attempt at nail art. I'm used to her intrusions so I barely look up when she comes in. When I eventually do, I can see she's pulling off her sweater and standing braless in the window. She puts a purple tanning mitt on her hand and turns to me shaking a bottle of false tan vigorously.

—And you're lucky you don't have to deal with all this crap yet.

She gestures to the pink and white bottle and turns back to the mirror.

Her breasts are full and I realise it's one of the first times I've noticed this. I look down at my own flat chest and rub my hand along my top, pressing out the creases.

—And there'll be time and all for those too.

I look up and see Saoirse eyeing me in the mirror. She cups her left breast with her gloved hand and shakes it, sticking out her tongue.

—Now, stop being a prepubescent pervert and come do my back.

I slide the mitt onto my fingers and Saoirse pumps brown foam onto the soft material.

—Don't leave any streaks.

I slide the foam across her back, massaging her skin and watching as her pores soak up the product. I run my hand across her shoulders, noticing the blackheads that cluster the area where her bra straps rest. I sweep my hand down to her lower back, feel the deep alcove of her spine and run my hand over the flesh that sits at the top of her grey jogger bottoms. When I'm done she pulls the mitt from my hand and holds it under her armpit, presses her palms against her nipples.

—I'll come for my sweater when I'm dry.

She leaves the room, door swinging, but just as I start to shout

—Close the door,

she hooks her ankle around the door and slams it shut, imitating me in a high-pitched voice.

—Clooooose the dooooor Saooooirse.

I go back to my nail art but notice a blob of tan on my wrist. I rub it and watch the soft skin change colour.

And I smile.

We didn't celebrate my sixteenth birthday because Saoirse died when she was sixteen and her little sister passing her out, her little sister suddenly becoming the older sister was too much for my family to handle.

It was probably too much for me to handle as well but part of me wanted a celebration. Part of me wanted to feel normal, feel like I mattered, feel that Saoirse being taken from us didn't mean that I was gone too.

We didn't celebrate any of my birthdays going forward so each year I had my own ritual. I sat and I ruminated.

When I turned twenty-one I thought about Saoirse. I thought about her love for men and romance, how each new boyfriend had brought her such excitement and joy.

I imagined what it would be like if she were alive. Would we have ended up sleeping with the same type of men? The same men?

The type of men I attracted: faceless. Soulless. After shared bottles of wine on late summer evenings. After words of affirmation or acts of affection. After lies and coercion. After bullshit and manipulation. I wondered if she would wake up in the same type of bedrooms on the same mornings after the same kind of nights out. I wondered if she'd too grow jaded, exhausted by these men.

YOU

I want you to feel the emptiness, the loneliness, the desperation. I want these stories to sink their teeth into you, pull you apart, pull your flesh asunder, open you up and leave you bloody and exposed to the elements. I want you to hear the sadness, the mourning, the grief. I want you to see the bodies pile up. I want you to question it all. I want you to drop to your knees and cry out and beg me to stop but I want you to keep listening. I want you to hear it all because you have to, you need to.

After you left there were moments when I was lost, completely. And in those moments, I let my body take over. It was lust and desire. It was adrenaline and addiction. It was distraction. I'd wake in a depression, you know the feeling, like there's a weight on you, like the air is filled with sand and you can't get up, can't get through it. And I'd lie there, in the dark, in the light, day, night and I'd touch myself and you'd flash before my eyes. You. Or him. Anybody. And I'd imagine my body, naked, bent over or laying back. And I'd touch myself, first slow and soft, then hard and fast and I'd climax to the image of a hand on my throat or fingers pulling my hair and then I'd feel powerful, you know, in the aftermath. In the glow, I'd feel woman again. I'd feel in control. Until then, when my body let me down, when my body betrayed me and the tears fell from my eyes, hot and slow.

But sometimes that wasn't enough. Sometimes I had to go further. And it was easy, you know. I sent a text, I set a time, I got a taxi halfway across the city to take off my clothes and feel a man push his body against me. And I went for the really fucked-up ones. The men who wanted to do weird shit. The men with girlfriends, the men with fetishes, the men who had no respect for me. That was imperative. The less respect the better. So I'd get on top of a man I secretly hated and I'd fuck him and love it. I fucked him until he came and then I'd won, something. I watched his face change, his body contort and I'd caused that, I'd made that happen. Then I got off and I got dressed and I left and I didn't feel happy or validated or satisfied, no, it was much better than that because when I left that shared house on Mountjoy Square or his parents' two-bed in Sandymount, what did I feel? Well, I didn't feel a fucking thing.

And the not feeling was the prize. The lack of warmth or love or even the lack of tears, this was what I chased, this feeling of pure emptiness. And I'd go home and I'd sleep well knowing that I could be that intimate, that vulnerable without feeling anything at all.

THE OTHERS

Then there were the others, the floating voters. The men who came and went. The now and agains. The back and forths. The on and offs.

The men who took me in at 4 a.m., mascara smeared across my cheeks.

The ones who came to me when they were kicked out by their girlfriends, or their wives or their friends or their mothers.

The ones who leaned on me or held me up or held me down or just held me.

The men who were confused but always smiling.

The men who said the right things at the right times.

—You're beautiful.

—You're funny.

—You're lovable.

—You're not a slut.

All the things I wanted to hear before I slept with them. And I always slept with them.

And I slept against them or in their arms. And I kissed them and I held my breath and I closed my eyes and I woke up and I let myself out and I didn't have to think about the night before.

And these relationships were defining. I suppose. In a way. But these relationships were the ones I kept quiet, to myself. Embarrassed or ashamed.

And I knew these men, I knew them better than I knew myself. In ways. In those non-committal, void of emotion ways. I knew their bodies, knew the shape of the words in their mouths, knew the smell of their desire. Knew their names and their exes, knew their highs and their lows. Knew parts of them that even their closest friends didn't know. But there were aspects of these men that I didn't know too, that I would never know. I didn't know what they did when I left. Didn't know if they washed the sheets or washed themselves or lay in the deluge of our intimacy.

I didn't have an awakening. Or I mean, I did, but I didn't remember it. Not properly. Not like the way other people did. Girls who could describe how their stomach felt the day before they got their period or knew where they were the first time they'd had an orgasm.

I didn't have a memory like that.

I didn't remember it like that.

I just woke up with a sense of knowing one day.

No, obviously not.

But, yes, kind of.

It felt like one day I was covering my mouth and laughing at boys' advances and the next I was straddling a boy in his apartment in Mountjoy Square.

And that's how it happened. In my mind.

And that was a lie. Obviously.

But this new me. This me that didn't believe in love any more. This new me who didn't want a relationship or a Valentine's card or a tattoo of someone's name on my arse, she couldn't remember the girl that had felt a jolt of jealousy in her stomach when Johnny Casey fingered Sheila Ryan against Lar Casey's car. She also couldn't remember the girl who had recoiled under Dave's father's fingers. This new girl, woman, she called the shots. She took her top off, she posed in front of men. She lowered then she got up and she left, and she buttoned her coat as the door closed behind her.

YOU

What you did felt loud and noisy, it broke the silence that cocooned us. You spoke the words and they were a gristly sinew getting caught in your teeth and the flesh of them rotted in your mouth and your breath was sour as you breathed on me and it made my eyes water and my stomach churn.

Your skin changed colour and your pallor resembled that of a ghost. I could almost see through you, could almost see past the lies and the hurt but soon you were opaque again and the reality hit me harder than your unearthly form ever could.

You reached out with words, apologies and the sounds landed neatly and I effortlessly brushed them away with the rough movements of the back of my hand and I scrubbed at my eyes to rid them of the sight of you.

—It's over Charlotte. I've met someone else.

Sometimes I just lie here and feel the loneliness surround me. It's my shroud and I feel safe in it. The quiet keeping me awake, keeping me alive. And the bed is always cold, always feels cold on your side so I run the palm of my hand along it and the emptiness is a kind of relief.

I read something about how in letting go you have to truly feel the absence first and that's what I'm doing, I'm feeling the loss of you and there is some sort of solace in that.

Your absence is present now. I stand in the mirror as the morning light casts blocks of yellow onto the floor and I can't see you, your uneven shape on the bed behind me, and the not seeing you could make me lose hours.

I continue to work because I have to, because that is the right thing to do. I continue to work because you are working, with her. I cannot let you win. I cannot let her see me fall to pieces, let her see my career crumble in my hands. She'll know of course, because you will have told her, how I hate teaching, but I won't have it said that you are the reason I quit. Besides, going there every morning and looking at the spotted faces of overindulged South Dublin youths doesn't feel any worse now than it did when we were together.

The kids seem to respect me more lately though, they look at me now with, not a tenderness or an empathy, but with an understanding and I know why. It's all because of a third-year class on *Romeo and Juliet*. One of the girls in the class posed an intelligent question.

—Why did Juliet kill herself?

And I'd replied, voice uninterested and cold

—I don't know, I suppose if she'd known the prick was alive she'd have killed him instead.

It made no sense of course but it got a laugh. It got too much of a good reaction and I'd sat up sharply at my desk afraid the laughter or the story would make its way to the principal's office. So I spent the next month trying to undo the damage, the moment that had caught me off guard, but the students looked at me differently now and word travelled to the other classes.

—Miss Murphy thinks Romeo is a prick.

Sometimes they catch me staring out the window, scribbling lines on the book in front of me. A student will have to raise their voice, say my name a few times before they get a reaction and I see the irony of it, the student telling the teacher not to look out the window. But I was never a good teacher, you know that. I was never interested enough to fulfil my duties, to instil a passion for the arts into these upper-class kids who already have jobs lined up in their daddies' firms. But then what if I had? Would I really push them to pursue English, do a degree that gave them no job prospects other than sitting in a class-room staring back at former versions of themselves?

At any rate I don't, and Romeo was a prick. He had to be, he was a man.

Some mornings I forget. I wait for the touch of your hand on my back or on my side, the sound of your voice in my ear or the light whir of the coffee machine or the shower, some-thing that signals your presence. Some mornings I wake knowing, I feel the cold of the room, the vacuum you've created.

Other mornings I do not think at all, I keep my eyes closed, searching for my dreams, racing towards another reality. But eventually I have to face you and the lack of you. Whether it's the surprise of an empty kitchen or the mirrors in the bathroom free from steam, I will have to walk into the day with acceptance.

I pull a blouse from my wardrobe and bring it to my face, smell the fabric that's sewn tightly at the armpit, always a muted, sour smell. I put it on regardless and spray perfume across my chest, then I pull up a navy skirt or a black one and I do the buttons and it hangs off my body and creases in the middle. I drag a brow pencil along my eyebrows and spread pink gloss across my cracked lips. I run my finger through my hair and then I pick up my KeepCup, put the lid on and sip. I burn my tongue and I leave the house with a burned mouth, and a cold body.

The journeys are short, back and forth from the apartment to the school, but the classes are long, drawn-out affairs and I feel myself age with each passing hour. In the staffroom the teachers speak about students and field trips and sports days but mostly it's idle chatter that comes from news headlines and there's a stale smell of packed lunches and bananas. I go out for lunch now, down to the café on the corner, mainly to escape the other teachers, the questions, the assumptions. I always failed to see the excitement of looking at Barbara Corkery's twins on her iPhone through a broken screen, or watching Desmond Holden rubbing his hands together and telling us how much he'd won on a horse at the weekend. But before, when you were still here, I could at least find some enjoyment in listening to the tales of their mundane lives because I was coming home to tell you. I loved telling you about Barbara's bad photography and the fact that one day she skipped too far ahead, and I saw a photo of her tits that I expected was for her husband.

Now I go to the café, and I order the blandest panini and I sit with it, and I don't eat and I watch as the time goes by. Then I go back to the school, to the evening classes and I see the students lose focus, become uneasy and I imagine myself in their place, looking up at the whitened face of a depressed teacher in a sour-smelling blouse.

They say memory is dangerous and I agree, our minds hold memories like a photo album and we see the good times clearly, smiling families holding new arrivals, brides in white dresses and ice creams to lips and sand on toes. Our memories try to repress the bad times and I suppose that's good, nobody wants to flick through an album filled with spilled wine and broken glasses, nobody wants to be reminded of the harsh words, the low blows, the shallow cries. But that's the wonderful thing about memory, even the repressed images can be brought back to us.

My memories of us are mainly good and it's these memories that make me weep, make me hold my knees to my chest and rock myself like a child. The good memories fill me with longing, they are vivid and loud and they play out in my mind as a cinematic reel. I watch them over and over and I wait for the rolling credits but when the credits come, I am asleep.

But there are bad memories too because nothing in life is perfect and you, as we have learned, are not perfect. And you couldn't be and it was unfair of me to put that on you, to venerate your perfection because that was an unrealistic expectation and for that, I suppose, I am sorry.

CON

—BTW, I delete everything when the conversation is over. I'd like you to do the same.

—Sure, of course.

—I exploded in the shower.

—Were you thinking about me?

—You know I was.

In a way, Con was the most vulnerable. He had so much to lose.

—Be my little slut?

—I will.

We met in Mary's, I was eating taco fries from the chipper next door and I'd had four pints. It was Friday evening and I was still in clothes from work, hadn't washed my hair. Con's friend was chatting up Mikala, but I was in no mood for flirting. I was facing away, chips balancing on the ledge behind us.

—So, is this like your regular?

I roll my eyes.

—We come here a bit after work, yeah.

Mikala is being polite, probably.

—So you guys are like work colleagues then?

I spin around.

—Sisters actually.

—No, we're not.

Mikala looks at me sharply.

—Are we not though?

I raise my eyebrows, rubbing taco sauce off my chin, and I catch Con looking at me.

—We could be, you know, if you were into that.

Mikala punches me.

—For fuck's sake Charlotte, shut up. I'm sorry. She's awful.

I pick up the chips and offer them out. The friend declines but Con takes a handful and puts them all in his mouth in one go, staring straight at me.

—I'm getting another drink.

When I get back from the bar they're talking about *Love Island*.

—I mean, it's addictive.

The friend gives his tantalising opinion on the subject.

I place my pint down and shimmy onto the high chair, adjusting the long fabric of my skirt so that I flash a small amount of upper thigh in the process.

—What do you think Charlotte?

Con looks right at me. He's learned my name. Mikala and her big mouth.

I take a long sip of my pint.

—I'm not sure. I feel the producers pick, like, emotionally vulnerable women.

Con raises his palms.

—As opposed to?

—Sorry?

—All women are emotionally vulnerable. In my opinion.

I give it a minute. I can see him trying to disguise the grin.

—Ah, the opinion of the small-minded, privileged white male. Nice.

—*I'm going to fuck her tonight and pretend it's you.*

—*Could just fuck me tonight?*

—*I will. In time.*

It was the boring friend who let it slip that Con was married.

—Show them the kid Con.

I hated him. But Con had just smiled and passed his phone around. I looked at the child smiling up from the screen. He had Con's eyes.

—Where's your wife tonight then?

I was suddenly ballsy. I was suddenly the one instigating this.

—At home with their kid I'd imagine.

I wanted to tell the friend to fuck off, the question had been addressed to Con, but I didn't. I didn't want to come off bitter.

—Yes indeed, and that's actually where I have to go now too.

—Is that your Instagram?

Mikala is still cradling Con's phone, ogling the baby.

—It is.

—Oh my God you should see Charlotte's, she's a real Insta whore. There, you're following her now.

I swipe the phone from her hand and pass it to Con.

—So sorry, just unfollow, please.

He looks down at his phone and then locks it.

—It was lovely to meet you ladies.

As he leaves, dickhead friend in tow, Con turns around and smiles at me.

It started off as fairly innocent sexting, then it escalated to videos and photos. He wanted me to sleep with other men and tell him about it, so I did.

—*Where did he touch you? Did you fuck him in the bar or did you take him home?*

He was obsessed with me fucking in bars. Sometimes I'd pretend.

—*In the cubicle, he had me up against the door.*

—*Did you cum?*

The texting was constant. In the morning he'd ask me to touch myself and tell him about it. At lunch he'd get me to take photos of myself in the bathroom.

—*I want to hear you. When you're with another man. That's what I want.*

I'd take a guy home and call him, leave the phone on my bedside table and let him listen.

I didn't really stop to think about her. I mean, this was never about her. But every now and then she came into my mind. His wife.

—*I think maybe I hate you.*

—*Does that make you want to fuck me?*

—*I think so, yeah.*

I had no idea what I was doing. There was so much excitement and resentment, it was all muddled together and I decided the best thing to do was ignore it all.

—*I want to feel myself inside you. I want to feel how wet you are for me.*

Obviously I never thought I'd do it. I mean, I couldn't, surely? He was married. He had a kid.

—*She's putting him to bed and I'm in the bathroom, touching myself over you.*

But I was in love with the moments. The befores and afters. The sighs, the looks, the silence. The moment when all was done and I pulled my tights on and he fixed his shirt and he always said 'are you okay?' like he thought I wasn't. Like he thought maybe I couldn't be. And then maybe I wasn't. There was nothing okay about this. This was far from okay but I felt safe, if that's what he meant. I felt safe with him and I knew we would be okay, even if what we were doing wasn't.

Did he love her?

And what did he think of me? At twenty-five, was I this young, easily influenced thing or had he built me up as some sort of fantasy? The texts were explicit and vulgar and felt, somehow, dirtier than the acts themselves.

—You've gone shy on me.

He'd say it, half in me, arms gripping my legs tight around his waist. And he'd be careful what he'd say then, afraid to insult me or take it too far.

I avoided his eyes, avoided looking at his face. What was I scared of? Feelings? Or just knowing too much of him. Like I didn't want to be able to identify him in a line-up.

I think we were both in denial, for a long time. It had started out as fun, risky, dangerous, exciting. But after a while it became something more, not the relationship but the consequences.

Did he love her?

Suddenly this mattered.

The first night I came to the office I felt sick. I didn't know what I was doing.

—*Are you going to get weird after?*

—*What does that even mean?*

—*Are you going to make my life difficult?*

—*You're clearly well able to do that yourself.*

—*But will you turn into a bunny boiler?*

—*No, Jesus, you've got a really elevated sense of self-worth don't you?*

Con was working late and I got a taxi to him. I couldn't find the entrance and he had to come down and open the door, find me. He acted so normal and as we walked up the stairs I noticed that strong country accent and this was something that was going to throw me time and time again. It was so far removed from his text personality.

We walked through the office. I commented on the interior and then we stopped at what I presumed was his desk.

These were the moments I lived for. The seconds. Standing, watching Con turn on the small desk lamp, make small talk as he cleared away books and paper. I let my coat fall to the floor.

—I didn't think this would happen.

I look away, reach out and catch the buckle on his belt. There is no kissing, he'd made that clear.

—*Cool, like a prostitute then.*

—*It's just better that way.*

His hands pull my waist towards him and before I can undo his jeans he's turned me around, pushed me over the desk.

—You're not wearing underwear.

—I know.

He pulls my skirt up and rubs me with one hand, the other fiddling with a condom.

—It's safer, you know.

I don't reply and he enters me, holding my hips tight.

YOU

When I'm alone, which is often now, I sink into myself. I find that vacant spot, the spot you once filled, and I enclose myself. I wrap around myself, enfold myself, embrace myself. I feel myself. I feel my neck and my chest, my breasts and my belly. I move my hands to my legs, between my thighs and I discover myself. I close my eyes and I try not to think of you.

There was a time, a long time ago, in my virginal state, when I could close my eyes and not think of anyone or anything. I could move with myself, the beat of my body, the pulse of my veins and the drum of my heart. I could shut down the buzzing in my head and instead feel a deep and pleasant tremor in my body. And the tremor would take me somewhere, somewhere a fire was burning, glowing, and pulsing. And I would follow it, move along the vibrations to find it, to see it, to touch it, to bask in its warmth. And I craved it, and it was beautiful, and it was comforting, and it was all mine to find and experience alone.

And I was a world unto myself in those moments, removed from the bed I lay in, the family I was part of, the school I attended and the body I inhabited.

I was floating. I was far away. I was safe.

But then I started to share it. I opened this space to teenage boys and men. I opened it to my mind and tried to understand it. I tried to make it palpable and functional. Easy and effective. Normal and communal. And the fire was moving further and further away, it was becoming a distant burning, a faint flicker in the night.

But I still saw it and felt it. Fainter now but still burning.

I still see it and feel it.

But now to get to it, now I must always think of you.

CON

Con had an intern. She was twenty-two. He talked about fucking her. He told me all about her. He wanted to show her what an older man could do. He wanted me and her to fuck him at the same time. I assumed he was all talk.

I wasn't expecting him to call that night.

'We're in the Jar, come meet us for a drink. I have that thing for you.'

There were so many questions. Who was he with? What had he told them? Was this safe?

Of course, I'd already signed up to this. I'd already put my morals to bed and I just went. Curiosity? Desperation? I don't know but I went. And it was the night that changed everything.

I got a taxi to the bar and when I arrived I sat in the back seat unable to open the door.

—You getting out love?

I apologised, flustered, pulling a tenner from my pocket, not waiting for change. I stood on the street and felt the wind curl up around my legs, dip beneath my coat and billow it outward. I looked at the door and wrapped my arms around myself. What was I doing?

Mikala had asked me why I was living like this.

—Do you want to be a cliché, is that it?

I didn't. But I guess I liked the attention, the excitement. She was the only one who knew, I couldn't tell anyone else. I'd tried to tell Pauline, who was living in Berlin now, had texted her, set it all up.

—*There's this guy, he's married.*

She'd immediately shut it down.

—*Well obviously that is absolutely disgusting and ridiculous. And obviously you're not going to pursue it.*

—*No. Obviously.*

She didn't understand, I told myself. But what didn't she understand? I couldn't explain it, not even to myself, and nobody seemed to think it was okay. Anything else I did was greeted with laughter and intrigue.

—God you're a mad bitch.

—Did you actually do that?

—No way?

But apparently an affair was where people drew the line. People were fucking fickle if you asked me.

—You going in love?

A man is standing too close, arm reaching over me for the door. Why is everyone calling me love tonight? I want to tell him to fuck off but that seems a little unfair.

—Yeah alright, calm down.

I take a breath and step inside the belly of the beast. I see him, sitting in the corner, at a table with two guys and a girl. His head is held over a pint and the silver strands shine in the half-light coming in through the window. I'd never noticed that before, the grey. He looks up and laughs at something being said, pats his hand on one of the guy's backs. Then he sees me.

He smiles and I feel nervous now. I brush my hair back from my eyes and look down. I feel like a girl, innocent, naïve. He gets up and walk towards me, arms out, and pulls me into a friendly embrace.

—I've said you're a friend of Maura's, an old colleague of mine.

It doesn't make sense, it's stupid. He's stupid. This is stupid. We walk back to the table and that's when I notice her properly, the intern.

—Clara leaves us tomorrow so this is farewell drinks.

He raises a glass to Clara after introducing me to the table. I look at her and I no longer feel young and innocent. I feel old, wise and outraged. She's pretty, plain but pretty, and wears a grey cardigan, much too old in style, and a skirt that sits just above the knee. She will never fuck him. But that's why I'm here.

He moves his hand onto my leg beneath the table. I'm wearing tights because I know he likes them, and I am pathetic like that. His hand moves further up my leg as he talks about his time in London and all the places that Clara must visit.

I put my hand on his and push it away. This is risky, too risky.

—I'm getting a drink.

He follows me to the bar and places his hand on the small of my back.

—What do you think?

—I think you're fucking crazy, that's what I think.

I say it through clenched teeth but he just grins back at me.

—She's cute though, right?

—She's a child Con, a bloody child.

I order a gin and tonic and he pays, which makes me uncomfortable but I'm too stressed to put up a fight.

—Thank you.

I hold the goblet to my lips, discarding the straw and gulping.

—It's okay, we don't need to do anything.

We go back to the table and for some reason he keeps looking at me, keeps pulling me into the conversation. He puts his arm around my shoulder all friendly and smiles.

—So how was your day?

We've left the conversation now, the others speak around us but Con only wants to speak to me. His eyes stare deeply into mine and although I am sure that I hate him, I like it when I'm with him.

—Do you want to come pick up those bits from the car then?

He says it loudly so that everyone can hear.

Con doesn't bring his car to work, his wife uses the car to drop their kid to school, surely everyone here knows this, but he just pulls on his jacket and finishes off his pint.

—Yeah sure, cool.

I literally do not know what else to say.

We leave in a flurry of goodbyes and good lucks and nice to meet yous.

I push the door open and feel the cool July air hit me in the face. I breathe it in.

—My office is just down here.

He gestures around the corner like this is news to me.

—I know. You know that I know.

His smile is like a child, excited for a birthday, and nothing I say takes it away. Is it because he knows that no matter how mad or uncomfortable I am I will follow him? I will go up the stairs of his office, past the conference room and right down the back to his desk. That I'll sit up in front of his monitor and touch him and do whatever he says.

When we get the office he looks around before he opens the door. Is he checking the coast is clear? Is he making sure his wife and child aren't sitting there, waiting to surprise Daddy? I wonder what he'd say if they were but lies come so easily to him that I believe he could get out of it.

—Are you coming?

I turn around and he's standing inside the door of the office, beckoning me forward. At least he hasn't called me love.

When we get to the top of the stairs he starts undressing me. He's saying things but I don't hear, don't understand with all my thoughts coming at me fast and loud. Before I realise it we are in the conference room and there's a long glass table.

—Will we?

After, as I pull my tights back on and he cleans the table with Dettol wipes I see a man in the building opposite looking out his window at us.

—Con.

I whisper it and he looks up, looks to where I'm looking.

—Shit.

The man sees us both and retreats from the window.

—It's fine. I'm sure it's fine.

It is for me. I almost say it.

—I'll let you out.

—I'm okay. You clean up here.

As I go to leave he hugs me but he holds me longer this time and when I let go he's still looking at me.

—You're so sexy.

Then he lowers his mouth to mine and kisses me. I kiss back and then I pull away.

—Bye.

I say it hurriedly and I rush down the stairs. I call a taxi and as I stand on the street, wind blowing my trench coat roughly at my ankles, I wonder, does he love her?

YOU

I would half wake in the depths of night, when darkness was our shroud, when the warmth of your body tethered me to the Earth, when the air was thick and heavy and sleep was our narcotic. My limbs were tangled in yours, hair matted to cheeks, the taste of morning not yet on our tongues and I would kiss you, somewhere, anywhere, lips half-moving, reaching, and your body would respond, would mould to my body and kiss me.

You became muscle memory and your shape would float into my dreams, would be the ballast, keeping me from falling deeper into that imaginary world where witches and warlocks lurked and teeth crumbled and fell out.

Your presence was a night light, the crack beneath the door, the streetlamp through the curtains.

I was safe.

Now I imagine you, lying there, next to her. I imagine the way your body becomes her armour, your hands her sword.

Sometimes I'd put my fingers around your neck and hold you. Sometimes, while you moved inside me, my fingers clenched your throat and I moved so that my full body weight was on you. Sometimes I gripped you tighter, watched your face redden, heard your breath catch.

Sometimes, you liked it.

Sometimes you'd take my hands and bring them to your neck.

Sometimes you'd beg me to choke you, just a little, right before you came. And I'd tighten my fingers on you, watch your eyes roll back and I'd only loosen when I felt your slow release.

Sometimes I was slow to loosen my grip. Too slow.

CON

Mikala is chain-smoking, she keeps saying babe and complaining about men and how they're all the same and how we are all totally screwed. I nod and say mmhmm in agreement, not really listening. The Pornstar Martini has a bitter aftertaste and far too much syrup.

—You know they're all compulsive liars, I swear.

I twist my glass between my fingers, the orangey liquid swirls up to the rim and catches the foam. I bring it to my lips.

—Like we owe them something.

My denim jacket is far too light and I have to keep pulling it in around my neck for warmth.

—But that's Republicans for you.

I look up now, unsure where this last notion has come from. Is she testing me, to see if I'm listening?

—Fucking men. Am I right?

I say yes and raise my empty glass. We clink. I'm safe. It's not that I'm not interested, it's just my mind is preoccupied. Con's face keeps coming to me and I can't block it out even though I want to.

—You know these Pornstar Martinis are meant to come with a shot of prosecco on the side.

I put my glass, sticky to the touch, back on the crumbling beer mat. The sun has dropped out of the sky and rows of twenty-somethings huddle together under the heaters and the dim light of the Pygmalion outdoor terrace.

—They put a shot of prosecco in the glass.

—I know, but they're meant to serve it on the side, in a shot glass.

I keep seeing his face, looking down, sullen as he pulls his trousers over his knees.

—We have to stop this.

I'm leaning out his office window smoking some shitty Pall Mall that Cian left in my coat pocket. I turn around, cigarette propped between two fingers held beside my eyebrow.

—Sorry, what?

—You know I hate when you smoke.

I make a gesture with my hands that indicates my lack of concern.

—I think we should . . . I know we should . . .

He's quiet as he buckles his belt and he looks at the floor. I turn back to the window and inhale the cigarette deeply. I make a scoffing noise as I feel my eyes starting to well.

—Whatever.

I say it and fake a laugh, but I can hear him move towards me and I hitch myself up higher on the desk, closer to the window. I can feel the night air kiss my face.

—Charlotte.

He touches my back softly.

I keep smoking, don't turn around.

—Look at me. Throw that down, you don't even smoke.

I spin around at that.

—Like you fucking know me.

I throw the cigarette out the window and slam it shut. I slide down from the desk but Con catches me and pulls me close. Then he smooths my hair out of my face and lifts my chin with his fingers. I feel childlike now, vulnerable. I don't look at him, not yet. He moves his face so close to me that when he speaks, I feel the words crawl across my skin.

—I'm sorry but we knew this day would come. It's gotten too risky.

I look up at him now.

—And whose fault is that?

—It's not . . . there's nobody . . .

—I have to go.

I push him backwards and escape his grip. I pick my bag up from the floor and leave the room. As I make my way to the stairwell I pass the conference room and see the glass table, I look out the window but the man next door isn't looking tonight, can't see my hasty exit.

Mikala shakes her bank card in front of my face.

—I *said* same again?

I apologise but she senses something is up.

—What's going on with you tonight?

She doesn't know about my last meeting with Con, or to be honest, our last five and I can't tell her now, I'll get that disapproving look and a lecture on how, imagine if it was me, imagine if I was the wife?

—Sorry, just a little drunk.

She looks at the two empty glasses in front of me and furrows her eyebrows, disbelieving.

When she comes back we cheers to asshole men and I drink the Martini much faster than the others. The DJ has started his set inside and there's a queue forming at the main door.

—So what about you?

Mikala uses her glass to enunciate her words and blue liquid from her Zombie cocktail spills onto the table in front of us.

—Oh you know, just Tinder, the usual.

—Yeah, but is there like, anyone in particular?

The night air sits on us now, cold, unforgiving and my jacket becomes stiff. I move it onto my shoulders to generate heat as Mikala pulls a packet of Pall Mall from her handbag. She leans back against the rope that separates us from the street and throws her head back, lighting her cigarette.

You'd think I would have seen her, the tall, beautiful woman approaching, you'd think I would have recognised her but I am oblivious to her movements right until there's a glass of white wine in my face. The liquid comes at me fast and it gets me in the eyes. I'm blinded and frightened for a second and I can hear Mikala cry out, feel her jumping from her seat. I pull my top up to wipe my face, feel the air on my stomach and when I open my eyes, I see Mikala stabbing the air with her cigarette in front of a tall, beautiful woman; another woman stands sheepishly behind.

—What the absolute flying fuck?

I don't need to look at her for long to know who she is. I've seen her before, seen her Instagram, her Facebook, seen her naked in their marital bed as Con filmed amateur porn and sent it to me.

—Mikala, it's fine.

I rub the remnants of Chardonnay off my nose with the back of my hand and I look at Con's wife, but I don't get up, don't feel the need.

—Aisling?

I say it like it's a question, but it obviously isn't. She looks back at me and she seems confused, sort of like she'd expected an outburst, a revolt. Then the confusion turns to sadness and I guess she was hoping I would deny it, hoping I'd put up a fight and she'd be able to pretend it was all her imagination, at least for one more night.

She takes a second and then responds. Her bottom lip is pursed, and I can see she wants to cry. She seems tipsy, not terribly drunk, and the empty glass hangs from her slender, manicured fingers.

—Who the fuck do you think you are, sleeping with my husband?

She leans over the table now, it seems like an aggressive move but I can feel her fear. I see Mikala slide back into her chair, mouth open, cigarette burnt right down to the butt, ash building at her fingertips.

—It's over.

I respond calmly, too calmly and I realise that I'm probably coming across like a psychopath.

—That's not what I asked.

And to be fair it wasn't. But suddenly I feel like I am in a movie, some terrible rom-com and I don't know what to say. I can taste the Chardonnay on my lips and I want to lick them.

—Look, this isn't the time or place. But I can tell you, it's over. He ended it.

She relaxes then and stands back up straight. I can't tell if it's tiredness or relief, but Con's wife stands up and puts the glass down.

—If you ever, ever come near my family again.

There's venom in her voice and I feel this sudden urge to hug her.

Her friend places a hand on her shoulder and starts to lead her away.

—Aisling,

I call after her as she turns her back.

She looks around, eyes wide, and I can see she has begun to cry. I forget why I've called her then. I stumble over my words, what were they, an apology? Instead, I wipe my mouth again and say

—He loves you.

She laughs and comes back to the table. She leans over me again and this time I feel no fear.

—Don't tell me what I already fucking know.

For a minute I think she's going to slap me and I kind of hope she does but instead she stands up, flicks her hair and leaves. I look at Mikala, she sits up straight in her chair cradling her glass. I can't tell what the look on her face is – anger, worry? I look at the table next to us and the one behind that. Everyone is staring, I can't tell what their faces say either.

—She slept with my husband.

She shouts it as she leaves the terrace and suddenly I know exactly what the faces say. I look down at my Pornstar Martini, the foamy top now destroyed with the rain of white wine. I pick it up and pour it onto the ground. I can feel everyone looking at me.

—It's meant to come with a fucking shot of prosecco on the side.

I shout it but I don't think anyone is listening.

YOU

I hold men in my hands, in my mouth. I feel their skin on my fingertips and my tongue. And these men, these complete strangers become muscle memory because bodies, in all their uniqueness, are really not unique at all.

Despite the fluctuations in tempo, temperature and taste, the body responds the same.

The body warms.

The body rises.

The body anticipates.

The body devours.

The body is so easy to manipulate and control.

And these bodies are mine now, beneath me or above me or below me.

These bodies are more mine than my own, because my body, my body still belongs to you.

SOME RANDOM DUDE

It's 4 a.m., 'Teenage Dirtbag' is playing on my laptop and some guy has spilled red wine on the carpet and it seeps into the other stains, left by other men. Always with the fucking red wine.

There are cigarette butts moulting in the bottom of an expensive plant pot that never held a plant and it's stashed on top of the cupboard because I don't smoke but I also don't want this guy to know the truth. The truth that he is not the first man to pat the wine stain into the carpet, making it worse, not the first guy to say 'What a throwback' to this song, not the first guy to look into my eyes and somehow manage to see past the glaringly obvious pain that rests there, right on the cornea.

I get up and walk to the sink. I reach my hand up and take down the plant pot that sits above it. A naked woman emblazons the body of the ceramic. I put my fingers in and pull out a cigarette butt.

The guy, I don't know his name, looks up at me from his overly comfortable position on my couch.

—What you doing?

He looks concerned.

—Sometimes I smoke.

—Alright cool.

I put my fingers back into the pot. I pull out more broken cigarette dregs.

—But not really. Not much. Not often.

He looks at his phone then back at me.

—I usually just let others smoke, you know, let them smoke around me. Like the second-hand smoke won't kill me, because you know like, it fucking will.

—You can smoke now if you want to?

He says it like a question, and I can feel the air sour.

—Why, do you have a cigarette?

—Well no, I . . .

He looks at me deeper, maybe now he can see the pain, maybe now he can see past the low-cut top and the short skirt, the red lipstick and the dark humour, maybe now he can see because he's stopped thinking with his cock. Maybe. But maybe not.

I take a handful of cigarette butt and ash and start to cram it into my mouth and chew.

He sits up. I've got his attention now.

—Ugh, man, what are you like . . . that's funny and all but like . . .

I keep chewing, finger more cigarette ends into my mouth.

He stands up.

—Ah come on now that's, I dunno like, that's getting a bit fucking weird.

I stop chewing and look at him.

—Leave then.

I say it through mouthfuls and watch as the ash sprinkles onto my chest.

He hesitates for a moment, unsure what to do. On the one hand, I was a clear easy lay, on the other hand, I now appear unhinged and definitely taste like smokes.

I start to laugh then and I think that clinches it. Me, standing at the sink laughing out mouthfuls of cigarette ends.

He leaves and I turn and spit the butts into the sink. Gripping the basin, I scrub my tongue with the brush.

CON

It was not ideal to be the sole witness to the death of the married man you were having an affair with and it would have been okay, I'm sure, if I'd run away, jumped over the barrier at the DART station and down past the Science Gallery of Trinity College and across O'Connell Bridge and down by the Liffey, all in a direction not towards my house for fear they'd find me, for fear she'd find me. But I didn't. I stayed. I stayed and I stood and I listened as the screams rose around me, as the DART continued to move and clatter along the tracks only to come to a screeching halt twenty feet away with passengers pressing their heads against the windows, phones out, trying to see what they could. So I was in all of the imagery, the videos and photos of the event. My blank visage became the face of this disaster, at least to the men and women aboard the train; luckily the sad truth of the story, that the tragic death of Con Houlihan happened when he was out with his mistress, did not make the tabloid press. But I'd like to think if it had, they'd have put my face on the cover.

I hadn't intended seeing Con again, not after the incident in Pygmalion with his wife, not after the glass of Chardonnay had been thrown into my face but life doesn't always go the way you plan. About three months later he reached out via email. Where he'd gotten my email address I do not know. Perhaps he'd seen it on the flyers I left in random SuperValus around Dublin offering English lessons. Perhaps his wife had brought the flyer home, held it under his nose and said

—What do you think, will our son need extra lessons?

And then pointed at my name as he dropped to his knees and cried at her feet until she told him to get up again.

Perhaps.

His email was brief and vague.

—*Hope this finds you well. I've been thinking about you.*

I looked at it and closed my laptop and sat like this for an hour. Then I got up, put the laptop away and went to bed. The following day I looked at it again and the day after that and eventually I clicked reply and wrote

—*What is it? Are you pregnant? Yours sincerely.*

I imagined his face then, imagined the smile, the curve of his lips as he gave a faint laugh and I imagined his fingers typing the reply

—*I lost your number. I want to see you.*

I replied with my number and he texted me not long after. The conversation was brief and to the point and despite knowing, deep within my heart and soul, that I should not sleep with Con Houlihan, the married man with the four-year-old son and the wife who knew about me and had warned me away, I went and I met him and I slept with him.

I suppose 'slept with' is a misleading phrase. There was no sleeping, only quiet fucks in a closed office after dark. I told nobody because nobody would understand. I didn't understand. Nobody would forgive it because I couldn't forgive it but in giving myself, my body, to this married man I was pretty sure I hated, I felt something and that something felt like relief.

I did not repent nor ask for forgiveness. You cannot ask for forgiveness when you are not sorry and I was not. I felt guilt somewhere in my bones but the guilty feeling was very easily overcome by the other feelings that Con Houlihan made me feel. At the start of our affair there had been excitement – no amount of excuses or long deep looks at my traumatic youth or my toxic relationships could change the fact that when I first slept with Con I did it for the excitement. But the excitement wore thin and that didn't keep me coming to his empty office block in the evenings.

—Like I'm confused. What are you trying to do? Are you trying to make yourself like, relevant or something? Is that it?

Mikala hated it. She hated me for doing it and I couldn't change her mind. I don't know what she meant by relevant and I don't think she knew herself but that wasn't why I was doing it. I was doing it now because it was vengeance. In some dark place in the depths of me, I felt vengeance. Every time Con lifted my skirt, every time he said something degrading and bent me over I felt vengeance. I couldn't explain it, I can't explain it now but fucking a married man, in that moment, felt like getting my own back. But not on the women, not on all the women, all the Sheila Ryans, all the tousled-haired women, I wasn't trying to get my own back on them. Somehow, this sordid affair made me feel like I was getting my own back on the men. There was a brutal glaring irony to the whole thing, that it was a woman whose life I was destroying, but for some reason I didn't see it like that. Instead I sat back and chatted to my friends and work colleagues about men and their lack of loyalty and how you couldn't trust them and how they were all the same and I nodded and affirmed and said

—Oh if you only knew what I knew.

And then I told the story of the married man who'd sent me a DM on Instagram asking to fuck me and watch me fuck other men and everyone let their mouths hang open and stopped drinking their drinks and then shook their heads saying

—I'm not even surprised, I should be but I'm not.

Then Mikala would corner me inside the pub and press her finger into my chest and say

—You left out the bit where you said yes.

And I'd push her finger away and say

—What are you on about?

And she'd say

—The bit where you said yes Charlotte, where you said yes to fucking the married man on the glass table of his conference room.

And I'd shush her then and say

—Jesus Christ Mikala.

And she'd say

—Jesus Christ yourself.

I think that my affair with the married man was the start of the end of our friendship, that's when it all started to fall apart. Her father had left her mother for some young one and I think that's why it upset her so much. Or maybe she was just a better person than me.

—And you call yourself a feminist?

She spat it at me the night after the altercation in Pygmalion and I'd laughed back and said

—You don't know the meaning of the word.

Which was immature and untrue and when I fucked Con in the following months I heard her voice play out in my mind. With each thrust of Con's hips I heard

—And you call yourself a feminist?

And I never used that word again.

I lost respect for myself then, not that I had much to begin with but any amount of respect I had was gone and so I used that as another excuse to fuck Con Houlihan. I was spoiled now and no amount of apologising to myself or his wife or the Lord above could change that so I might as well keep it going. And I did and it got weirder and he got weirder and he started fucking his wife again, the wife he apparently hadn't fucked in over a year and he'd text me and he'd tell me how he'd imagined me while he was doing it. And I was intrigued now because he was so fucked up and I went along with it and Jesus, maybe I was fucked up too, maybe I am fucked up because I was disgusted and repulsed but when he sent me videos of him fucking his wife I touched myself and I came and then I cried myself to sleep.

YOU

I was scared.

   Scared of myself.

   Scared of you.

   Scared of them.

   Scared of late nights and dark alleys. Scared of chat-up lines and hands on shoulders. Inappropriate comments and grey-line crossing.

   Scared.

   Scared of the undeniability of my vulnerability.

   The fragility of my self-worth.

   The fragility of my sister's body.

   The identifying of my sister's body.

   The ease with which these men attacked. Devoured. Destroyed.

   The ease with which they controlled and manipulated.

   The TV screens. The news. The flashing bright lights of a police car.

   The holding up of a thong in a courtroom.

   The fact that I was to blame.

   That she was to blame.

The fact that I chased danger.

The fact that I not only couldn't escape but that I was unable to even try.

Scared of the people who could help because they were all men too.

They had all seen her and touched her and there were hands and fingers pulling and poking and prodding.

And Saoirse lay there and I reached out and I touched her and she was cold and the room was white and a streak of fake tan was still fresh on her forearm and I ran my fingers across it and still, I was scared.

SAOIRSE

I wake in the night, sweat cooling on my back. I can sense somebody in my room. I sit up. I see Saoirse at my mirror. She's laughing, pulling fingers through her hair.

—The lighting in this flat is appalling Char.

I sit up, my eyes adjusting to the darkness. Blood pumping fast through my veins, fingers shaking, reaching for my light switch, failing to find it.

Saoirse turns around, naked.

—Am I streaky?

She holds her arms down by her sides and opens out her palms. Blood pours from her hands.

—You're so lucky you don't have to deal with this crap yet.

I try to scream but sound catches in my throat.

I wake in the night.

My bed is wet.

YOU

And let's be honest here, it wasn't all bad. All the men, all the moments, all the experiences, well, they weren't all bad because how could they be? Even tragedy has its appeal, I guess.

So it wasn't all morbidity and abuse. It wasn't all cheating and lying and deceiving. It wasn't all pretending and confounding and denying. No, there were beautiful moments amid the wreckage. Moments where hands were held and kisses were shared and words were said and they made me smile, made me weaken, made me falter, made me love.

Yes, love. And I did love. I believe I loved. Not the person, not the relationship and not with a love that looked to the future nor a love that yearned for the past, no, I loved with a love of contemporality, I loved the present, the steadfast love of that moment.

I loved the regularity of love. The morning text. The late-night call. The midweek dates.

I loved the familiarity of love. My side of the sofa. His side of the bed. The smell of his t-shirt as the fabric rubbed against my skin.

I loved the way words would form on a lover's tongue and they were the same words I'd heard before but now they were reborn in a new accent, a rougher intonation.

I loved how ductile love was. How easily it could change and grow and bloom.

But this also meant that my love was capricious, flighty.

So for all this. All my love of loves, I had a sense of what was coming.

I guess, I had seen it all before.

SAOIRSE

The room is shrinking. The walls closing. Doors heavier and louder when they bang in the dark. My breathing is quick, shallow, it catches and I bolt upright, pulling at an invisible hand around my throat.

I see Saoirse in the darkness, often now. Her apparition is always the same, she's still a teenager, wearing the same outfit she wore the night she died. But even though she looks the same, she still appears younger to me now. My big sister, immortalised at sixteen.

Sometimes I talk to her, I tell her about leaving puberty behind, about becoming a woman. I tell her that my breasts finally came in and that my period came, the night she died, a weird synchronisation, my body bleeding alongside hers.

Saoirse died when I was twelve. She was six years older than me.

Saoirse was stabbed eleven times. Eleven. Not four or five. Eleven. They said she was probably dead by the third but I guess he wanted to be sure.

For a few years I was known as the girl with the brutally murdered sister but then Kurt Simmons let his daughter fall on a newly tiled kitchen floor and my story, our story, was forgotten. By the time I was fifteen and on the dating scene myself, nobody seemed to even mention my sister any more.

I thought about her often. I imagined her face, that white porcelain with dark shadows under her eyes. I thought about her hair, fine and dark, parted in the middle and her smile, far wider than mine, opening up, reaching both sides of her face. I thought about her touch and how she'd run her hand across my shoulder and pull me into an embrace before teasing me and pushing me away gently. I thought about her legs, longer than mine, taking up more of the bed and how her feet were cold when they touched me. I thought about her smell, the sweet lavender of the perfume that our grandmother had gifted her.

I could see her always, in my mind's eye, standing at the mirror in her bedroom, twisting the ends of her hair inwards with a hot iron. I would stand on one leg, the other wrapped around my ankle, staring at her as she patted red into her lips and looked towards me and winked. Then she'd place her lips against where the image of her cheek had been just moments before and the print would stay there and I would look at it in the mirror, run my finger along it.

She was forever having arguments with my mother. She was too young for 'rouge' and it wasn't until years later that I heard that word again and laughed, raising my hand to the invisible print left there by her phantom.

She told me he was perfect.

She told me he was tall and handsome and 'not that that stuff matters' but he was.

She told me this in a matter-of-fact way.

She told me he called her baby and that made me feel uncomfortable but when she sat at the bottom of my bed, patted my legs under my duvet and closed her eyes and said

—Oh, oh Charlotte, it's just, it's love,

I felt a sort of yearning, a deep need for this thing she spoke of.

And I never imagined that he would stab her once, twice or indeed eleven times in the chest.

I needed a sister. I needed a friend. I needed someone to help me navigate this journey. And my mother wasn't present, not really, not after Saoirse died and I needed a woman, I needed some female energy to show me how to be in this world. I needed someone to help me transform.

And I'm not trying to romanticise it, this growing up, this pubescent journey. Because it's not romantic, it's not glamorous. It's not trying on bras and comical attempts at shaving your legs. It's not learning how to insert a tampon or discovering how to kiss. It's so much more than all of that and those moments are just a mise en abyme. Those moments are just white noise, an electric buzzing in the background when the real noise, the roaring, howling noise of becoming a woman is all you can hear. And it's raw and it's vulgar.

It's inhabiting a body that has disowned you.

It's people looking at you and expecting things from you.

It's learning, not how to bleed once a month, but how not to bleed every single day. Bleed from your heart into your soul because it all hurts. It all moves and writhes and turns inside you. And I needed her, I needed my sister. I needed her to show me how to move in this new body. I needed her to tell me what to say to boys when they tried to put their hand up my top, when they told me they didn't like condoms, when they pushed my face into the pillow and held me there and used me until they were done. I needed her to plait my hair. I needed her to thread my brows. I need her hands on my skin to tell me I was beautiful.

And I couldn't romanticise it, this growing up because growing up, moving on was not an option. Not when she was taken from me. Not when he had taken her from me.

YOU

I pushed Con Houlihan in front of the DART. I pushed him to his death.

I pushed Kyle too. I pushed Kyle into the Liffey when he was so drunk that he could barely stand. And his arms flailed about, and he grabbed at me and I was tempted to reach out and touch him, one last time, to feel the softness of his fingers against mine, but then I remembered where his hands had been, and I remembered all of the nights that he had chosen someone else over me, and I'd let him go.

And getting rid of these men became easy and I learned fast, not that it was ever intentional, not that I went out of my way to kill these men, but still, I learned fast and I learned early. I learned how to cut the brakes in Lar's car from YouTube videos.

Adam was the easiest because I barely knew him. I put three ecstasy tablets in his rosé and he just looked like he was asleep.

And I held my fingers so tightly around Dave's neck as he moved inside me that he stopped breathing before he was able to cum. After, I hoisted his neck into the rope I'd fastened round the shower rail and looked at him hanging there, his dick limp.

And you look so beautiful now, with her. And I know that this is your favourite time of day, when you close the tattoo parlour, when you both cycle home and haul those stupid, awkward-looking bikes up the stairs to your flat on the third floor. I know this is the time of day you live for, the moments you cherish, the moments that she has stolen from me. The moments that were mine.

So I'm here love, in Waterford, outside your house and I'm here to take my moment back. This moment that could have been pre-recorded in our Dublin flat, but with me instead of this ridiculous stunt double.

I imagine her now, taking off her clothes as you drag a canvas out and hold a brush between your teeth, as I ascend your stairs, as I pass the stupid, awkward bikes. I hear her laughing, hear the clink of paintbrush against glass jar, feel the shape of the knife in my back pocket.

Oh what a painting this will be.

ME

The moments were like light coming through the darkness. Somewhere in the distance, a flicker and a feeling of warmth, the morning sun.

A text back.

A smile.

A hand on the small of my back.

I could blame Disney, I suppose, or my relationship with my parents or that boy who called me a slut in second year.

I could blame myself. I could blame my underactive thyroid, or my overactive libido, my addiction to coffee or the fact that I've always found it hard to establish solid relationships with other females.

I could blame it on any of those things but the truth is, I must blame it on that look a man gives, across a table, across a bar. That look that says hello, hi, come to me, be with me. I must blame it on the look followed by the touch, the caress of a man's skin against mine, the ease with which men come to me and the way I melt into them.

A man looks at me now, across the room as I sit, cradling this gin and tonic.

And in this moment I am seventeen again and I am standing in O'Donovan's holding a vodka laced with orange cordial
and I hate my body and my face and the awkwardness of it and
I feel every man's hands, fingers, lips and hips as they press
them all against me and I take them and I accept them and I
hate myself and my body and I imagine every time I'd let the
strap of a dress or a top slip from my shoulders and I regret
the confidence with which I'd done it, the unbuttoning, the
unzipping, the exposing. I feel the numbness creep into my
bones now and I see the faces of strangers that are familiar to
me. And these familiar strangers are all naked and sweating
and grabbing and pulling and I'm not seventeen now but I am
still awkward and shy and I want to scream and cry but I hold
it in.

I imagine wet sheets and pulled muscles, sweaty brows and
chapped lips. I imagine my body intertwined in theirs and the
warmth of their skin against mine. I imagine the loosening and
tightening, the push and pull, the smile on my lips. I want to
put my fingers there on my own lips, on that smile and pull it
wider from either side and rip it open, rip it apart and feel the
blood run down my fingers as my skin cracks open to reveal
my mouth and my teeth bore in a sort of sick grin. I want to
take my own head and smash it hard against the table that sits
beside the bed, the bed that holds memories of men huffing
and grunting and coming. Because I'm ashamed now and it's
not rational shame. It's a shame that comes from deep within,
a shame that was planted years and years ago, before I'd placed
my tongue in Johnny Casey's mouth or ran my hand along
Lar's hard cock. Before I lifted my skirt for a married man,
leaning with my palms down onto the glass of a conference

table. There's a seed of shame that came before the one-night stands, the fumbles in dark alleyways and this seed was planted before I was born and the plant is alive now and it is growing and it is sprouting and the branches are reaching out inside me trying to escape. But the shame is mine and it could not exist without me so I am left to hold it and carry it and grow around it.

He places his glass on the table in front of me.

—My name's Stephen. It's a pleasure to meet you.

I extend a hand.

—Charlotte. And no, the pleasure is all mine.

US

I reach out, into the darkness. It's warm here, because of the bodies. Arms and legs surround us. The heat of skin against skin, the slow undulation bringing us closer together.

I see Saoirse through the darkness, I see her and I feel her and soon we are wrapped in one another. As the stomach muscles move, as we are slowly churned and compacted.

Saoirse's arms stretch out and enfold me. I sink into her breast.

The breath of the women around us is deep, hot.

She strokes my hair. She is the big sister again and she will protect me.

We pull each other even tighter so our bodies mould together. We are one.

The man swallows. More women join us. The place is crowded now. There is not room for us all.

Slowly we start to disappear, one by one.

Saoirse and I melt into each other, into ourselves, into this man's body. We hold each other in the darkness.

My body.

Her body.

Their bodies.

One body.

ACKNOWLEDGEMENTS

This is long. I'm so grateful for the people in my life so please bear with me.

I don't think I'm alone in thinking that writing a book is a very bizarre endeavour. You spend a huge amount of time, possibly years, pouring a huge part of yourself into a project that may never actually see the light of day. I wrote *Bodies* in a vacuum. There was a pandemic and I had moved back in with my parents for a few months, shutting myself away from the world and writing, basically, how I felt. I was angry but I was also pretty lucid, a combination I was not really accustomed to and *Bodies* just kind of spilled out of me. Words, ideas, sentences, all falling onto a keyboard and forming a structure that I could almost see as a novel. I knew what I wanted to say and I was praying someone would listen. But at the same time and in a very real way, I genuinely didn't believe anyone ever would. Then someone did and then someone else and then, well, I was just like, damn, people are going to see this, my mother is going to kill me for all the swearing.

I want to thank Max in the first instance for not deleting your old email and for putting me in contact with Sara. You are a certified legend. Pints in Dublin again soon? I want to thank my wonderful editor Jocasta for your understanding of my vision and support during the rocky moments, and there were rocky moments, us artists are a difficult bunch and writing a book is hard, who knew? I want to thank all the team at John Murray for being so supportive, helpful and just generally cool. Thanks to the two Charlottes for all your work; how apt is my protagonist's name? I want to give an extra big thank you to my agent Sara for the endless support that surpassed all editorial and agent type stuff. Your belief in my writing was the driving force behind *Bodies* and you were always on the sideline making sure I didn't give up. You are not just my agent but a very dear friend.

To my secondary school English teachers, Eileen Moyles and Karen Spencer, thank you for always making me submit my writing to competitions and to the Duiske College girlies who always said I'd publish a novel. Thank you to Deirdre Madden and the Creative Writing department at Trinity College Dublin and to good old Trinity in general for allowing an awkward and slightly weird girl from the country to embrace who she truly was. I would relive those four years over a thousand times. To the Oxford University Creative Writing Department, thank you for helping me find my voice and for the continued support even now. And seriously, sorry for how hungover I used to be at residency, you gave us too much free wine! To the team at Curtis Brown Creative for helping me understand the industry and for always minding the personal belongings I left in your offices each week.

Now onto my friends. Buckle up, this is long. I only now realise I actually have lots of friends. Cool! To my dear friend

Zoe who acts as friend and therapist and who always responds to my chaotic dating story voicenotes with, 'this is why you are a writer, this is brilliant!' Thanks for always seeing the funny side to my trauma, it helps. To Kev Nev for being Kev Nev, my best friend, the best friend anyone could ask for. Thank you for literally everything. You know how much you mean to me and if I started to list all the reasons we would be here all night. To Matija for constantly getting me out of trouble and making me do better. They say there's no such thing as a free lunch but Matija has given me many. To Laura for your supportive and non-judgemental friendship. You are one of the most special people I know and I absolutely adore our long rants about everything and nothing. To Paget, my beautiful friend inside and out. Our friendship has lasted through continent moves and pandemics. I love you dearly. To Tony for always answering my calls and stopping me from spiralling. I am so happy we are friends. To Danny, thank you. I finally published *Fifty Shades of Ginger*, you'd be so proud of me. I miss you dearly. To Anil, thank you for being my Dublin Creative friend. Those late night rambles at l'Gueuleton helped me finish this book and that isn't even a joke. You are a very special and important person in my life. To my babe Colleen, thank you for coming to every single event I've ever read at. Thank you for listening to all my drama and giving sage advice. Sorry for being such a crazy manager back in the day but thank God we worked together. You've gone from '16hr contract Colleen' to one of my best best friends. You know how much you mean to me, you and your gums. To Oisin 'have you finished your novel yet' Flynn, thank you for making me finish my novel. And thank you for everything else, you know how much you've helped me. You've already inspired book two; time will tell if that's a positive or a negative. I love you lots and always will.

If you're still reading this you're probably mentioned here but if not, fair play for getting this far. These next people are the most important. To Joanne, my wonderful sister, thank you for carrying me to breakfast every morning until an age which would be embarrassing to state here. Thank you also for the academic help. But most importantly, thank you for being my absolute best friend (shared with Rebecca) all these years. I love how we share the exact same taste in TV programmes and fiddle faddles. To Rebecca, my other best friend. Thank you for all the ridiculous but very enlightening conversations about that pesky old patriarchy. Thank you for being my literal chaperone and thank you for comparing me to Donal Ryan that one time. We have the best adventures, and I couldn't imagine travelling around as much with anyone but you. To my little Butler family. Moll Doll, I love you. Joe, I love you too. And Michael, I love you like the brother I never had. I've dedicated this book to my grandparents and I hope that shows how much I love you all. To my late Granny and Grandad Foley, thank you for everything. To my Granny and Grandad Bridgett, thank you for everything. I hope to be as in love as you are when I'm your age. Granny, I'll never forget you forcing me to enter that radio short story competition and being so sure I would win. You were right. To my Auntie/second mother Ellen, thank you for everything you've done for me over the years. I love having you in my life.

Okay, we're nearly there, promise. Only three more acknowledgements. Thank you to Daddy for so much. Thank you for being my personal driver for thirty-three years. Thank you for literally jumping into the car and collecting me or driving me anywhere and everywhere, day or night. Thank you for coming upstairs to my room to ethically remove spiders at all hours. Thank you for (but also please stop) bragging about me to every man, woman or child we meet. Thank you for being so proud of me. I could not have done this without you. But mostly, thank you for being one of the few men who leaves me with faith in the sex. I love you. To Mammy, I left you until last because you are the main reason this book exists. Your belief in me has always been unwavering, despite the many mistakes I've made over the years. I don't know if I'll ever accept the fact that you are always right, but I can at least thank you for always bailing me out. Although your financial help has always been greatly appreciated, it's not what I want to thank you for. I want to thank you for your love and care. I want to thank you for being my real best friend (sorry everyone above). I look up to you more than you could ever imagine and I love you more than even I, the 'writer', can put into words. I can't imagine where I would be without you but I would not be writing the acknowledgements of my bestselling novel. (You said it will be bestselling, let's see.) I love you.

Finally, last AND indeed least, thank you to the men who helped shape this novel. Thank you for the gaslighting, the love bombing, the cheating. Without you this book would never have been written, you have made my dream come true. Seriously, thanks. And yes, I know you're reading this, this is like next level Instagram stalking and honey, I see you. Xoxo.